AUDITED
BY THE
Anubis

WENDI GOGH

Audited By The Anubis by Wendi Gogh

Copyright © 2023 by Wendi Gogh

All rights reserved.

ISBN: 979-8-8691-9109-0

First Edition: November 2023

Cover by Phantom Dame
Edited by Miranda Vaughan Jones

Monster Heart Ink
New York, NY

www.wendigogh.com

Printed in the United States of America

Chapter

One

FERN

Hell's bells—someone's at the door.

No one ever comes to visit me, especially on a Thursday afternoon. It's two o'clock, and Seraphina is at the bakery so that I can have the day off.

Thus far, I've spent it eating an absurd amount of Irish potato cookies and binge watching Bridgerton.

Why can't I have any wealthy men vying for my hand in marriage?

I remind myself that I'm not interested in said wealthy men because one marriage was enough for me.

The knocking on the door persists, and I groan. Unlike my phone, I can't silence my visitor. Another five minutes pass, and the person is still at my door.

Huffing, I unwind from my tangle of blankets and shuffle across my living room floor. My fleece socks crackle with the contact, my short red hair ballooning around my head.

Fairly certain I have enough electricity to power an off-grid community, I kick my rain boots as I pass them, hoping the rubber disperses the charge.

Peeping through the thin stained glass that decorates the sides of the front door of my Victorian house, I nearly fall over when I spy who's on my porch.

Tall, dark, and handsome?

Nuh uh.

More like tall, dark, and *deadly*.

A seven-foot monster stands there, waiting patiently for me to open the door that I have no plan of answering.

The black fur covering his face and snout is smooth and shiny, a contrast to his tail, which appears very bushy.

His large, soulful eyes are lined with gold, and there's a small hoop earring through one of his ears.

The navy suit he sports appears more indigo than blue when he steps back into the sunlight, and I spy the infamous ankh on his tie, along with a scarab beetle holding the sun of Ra.

Legend has it that the Anubis are descended from a literal god of death, but picking out truth and myth from monster origins is just about as tricky as doing it for humans.

But in this moment, with my breath fogging the stained glass as I stare at the magnificent creature on the other side of my door, I believe it.

This Anubis definitely looks like a god—or the descendant of one.

He clears his throat, one sharp, long, black claw tapping on his briefcase impatiently. Finally, he sighs.

"Ma'am, are you going to let me in?"

I squeak, tumbling back and crashing to the floor.

"N-nobody's home!" I stammer like an idiot.

Another sigh.

"Listen, I promise that you have nothing to fear. I come in peace."

Peace?

Maybe he's just an ardent follower of his God and trying to spread the good word. Either way, I can't very well go on pretending I'm not home and ignoring him.

With a wince, I climb to my feet, my ankle tender where I rolled and sat on it. I unbolt the locks and open the door a crack.

"Miss Fern Mabon?"

"That's me."

"I'm Ahnou Napa with the IRS—I'd like to talk to you about your taxes."

Letting the door fall open, I stare at the man in shock. Of all the things I expected him to say, this isn't it.

"Is everything all right?"

"Your EIN was flagged for auditing."

A shudder shakes my shoulders and rolls its way down my spine.

Audited—*a business owner's worst nightmare.*

Gulping, I step aside. "Um, please come in."

The Anubis has to duck underneath my door frame to get through, and when he straightens back up, his muscular form fills the tiny foyer.

Guy's larger than life.

My fingers grip my oversized sweater, twisting the fabric around the painted tips of my fingernails.

I'm in no way prepared to be audited—or for the presence this man brings.

"Can I get you some tea?"

"Thank you. How kind of you—" He pauses, his snout lifting straight into the air as he sniffs, the corded muscles in his neck going taut. "Are those cookies I smell?"

A wretched blush crawls up from my throat to my cheeks—the curse of being a redhead. "I…I ate them all."

I wait for him to say something snide, or at least snort while looking me up and down. It's patently obvious I'm thicker than I should be, even in my oversized shirt and pants.

Girls like me probably shouldn't plop down and eat a dozen cookies in one sitting—something my ex constantly berated me for.

But the Anubis only gives me a lopsided grin, baring the sharp whites of his canines. "If they were half as delicious as they smell, I can see why you ate them all."

My mind tries to piece together what he said, but it can't.

For the past five years, it's endured every cruel remark under the sun, but this one man's comment has scrambled my thinking abilities into mush.

He's just being polite, I hiss mentally.

Turning on my heel, I march into the living room, hoping he follows me. He does, and I gesture at my orange couch for him to sit down.

"I'll be right back with the tea."

A million thoughts buzz in my head like an angry hive of bees while I enter my kitchen and get what I need.

My hands shake as I place a cup and saucer on a fancy, silver tray—I tell myself it's nerves because I'm being audited, but deep down, I know it's more than that.

I'm drawn to this monstrously handsome being.

It's just because he didn't call you a fat cow.

With this depressing thought, I return to the living room. "Here we are, Mr. Napa." I set the tray down on the coffee table before him.

"Please, call me Ahnou."

The blush returns, and I want to smack myself in the face. He's clearly trying to put me at ease, *not* coming onto me.

"Ok, only if you'll call me Fern."

His black lips purse together. "Perhaps…if it's just the two of us."

My heart races.

Why did he make that sound so intimate?

"Am I in trouble?" I blurt out.

Maybe he wants me to use his first name to soften me up before he breaks the news that I'm going to tax jail.

Ahnou shakes his head, taking a sip of tea, but before he answers, his eyes flutter close. "This is *amazing*. What flavor is it?"

"Oh, it's a specialty—from my café. It's Orange Blossom Jasmine."

"It tastes like magic in a cup."

His words send my pulse into hyperdrive.

"Are you just saying that to butter me up before you tell me the bad news?"

The tea cup pauses mid-air between the saucer and his mouth. "What bad news?"

"That I'm in tax trouble."

"Ah. I should clarify that an audit is a routine procedure that the IRS does every year. People are randomly selected to ensure that taxes are being filed properly."

Relief crashes over me like a tidal wave. "Oh, I thought that the IRS only audited somebody when they were in trouble with their taxes."

"Sometimes, but not all the time."

"So this is only a routine checkup?"

Ahnou winces. "Miss Mabon—Fern—have you received any letters from the IRS?"

My face falls blank as I try to school my features into something that makes me appear semi-competent.

"Yes, of course, I received them."

"Did you read them?"

My stomach heaves as I fight the urge to throw up.

"If I can be frank, my mother handles my taxes."

Along with other things.

The giant man frowns before opening up his briefcase. He pulls out a pair of gold-rimmed glasses from his pocket that he perches in the middle of his long snout as he reads something.

They look so adorably perfect on him that I can't stifle the giggle that escapes past my lips. His head jerks up with an inhuman sharpness.

"Is something amusing?"

"N-no," I stammer. "It's just that your glasses make you look very studious—they're cute."

I clamp my mouth shut, my lips twisting into a grimace.

Shut up, Fern!

The Anubis only shoots me another lopsided grin that makes my heart flutter…along with other regions further south.

"I look like an old man with them on," he grouses, and I clap a hand over my mouth to stifle another laugh because *nothing* could be further from the truth.

He looks like a nerdy sex god sent from above to taunt me—or maybe it's from below.

"Fern, has your mother always done your taxes?" I nod, and he continues. "In previous years, it doesn't say that they were prepared by anyone but you."

"Oh, um, I mean my mom is my business manager, and she's always filed them for me. Like on my behalf…so it was me but not. Wow. I sound like an idiot."

I mutter this last part under my breath, glancing down at the floor as abject embarrassment consumes me.

Ahnou leans forward, one of his sharp black claws tipping my chin upward. "You're *not* an idiot.

Owning a business is no small task, and there are many rules and stipulations that can be overlooked or forgotten.

The IRS understands this and adjusts for it. I'm sure it never occurred to either you or your mother for her to say she prepared your taxes since she is not a legal tax preparation company."

I swallow, my body tingling in awareness at his touch. "O-okay, good."

It's the best I can manage under the circumstances. Finally, he breaks contact, and I sag back into the couch, relieved yet bereft.

"So is that the only thing you needed to check up on?"

My voice raises up at the end, betraying my inner anxiety worse than the blush that scorches my face.

"I'm afraid not. The real reason that you were flagged for an audit is because your taxes haven't been filed in over two years."

A chuckle that sounds more like a hysterical cackle bursts free of me and echoes around us.

"That's not possible!"

Ahnou takes off his glasses and shoots me a sympathetic look. "I promise you, I'm not lying to you."

This time when my stomach revolts, I know there's no holding it back.

"Please excuse me while I go make a phone call."

And by phone call, I mean puke.

Chapter

Two

AHNOU

Welcome to Cedar Peak Heights!

The sign elicits a chuckle from me. This far east in Virginia, the tallest peak around was likely an anthill anyone could piss over.

But humans were oddly territorial as they were sentimental. If one part of Virginia boasted mountain tops and panoramic views, then the whole state would.

Clearly the folks of Cedar Peak Heights decided to go big with the town's name since they had nothing else to compete with the state's western topography.

Which is a shame because the deciduous trees here might be some of the most gorgeous fall foliage I've ever seen.

For a town of just under five thousand residents, it has plenty of stores and restaurants. One in particular stands out—Sugar and Spice café, owned by my current auditee.

From the outside, it looks warm and inviting, the window bedecked with autumn decor in vibrant reds, yellows, and oranges.

In less than five minutes, I'm pulling into Miss Mabon's driveway, and I wish my job was only moments away from where I lived.

Even though I'm a homebody, I spend over half the months in the year away doing audits. How I long for my own bed and kitchen—eating out gets old after a few weeks.

But I still have three more audits to finish this year before I can return to my house.

I contemplate the stately house while collecting myself. As an introvert, doing these yearly audits almost makes me want to quit my job.

One would think working for the IRS would be spent sitting in a cubicle, pouring over tax forms for hours.

It's not—something I learned the hard way.

Not all IRS employees perform in-person audits, but the government thought with me being a monster, I would be a good representative to knock on *other* monsters' doors.

Except in the five years that I've been doing this, I've only audited two monsters—all the rest were human.

Whether the IRS doesn't realize that the combination of being audited and by a monster is a disaster in the making, or they just don't care, I don't know.

But it certainly doesn't make my job any easier.

One woman thought I was actually there to mummify her. I jokingly told her that I left my Canopic jars at home…

She slammed the door in my face, locked it, and refused to open it again. The IRS had to send someone else to audit her.

At this point, you think the government would've wised up, but they didn't. And here I sit, ready to traumatize some other poor soul.

It takes me a moment to unfold myself from my tiny electric car. I love that I'm helping cut down on Earth's carbon footprint, but wish they made these things bigger.

Even for a monster, I'm fairly large.

Straightening my suit jacket and tie, I step onto the porch. The wood groans under my weight, but holds, and I hope the structure is sturdier than it looks.

Because the only thing worse than being audited by a monster is one that breaks your house.

With a deep inhale. I rap on the door and wait. My keen hearing picks up on the sound of a television set, but that doesn't necessarily mean that someone's home.

People leave their TVs on all the time for their pets.

I knock again, and this time I hear a distinctive feminine murmur. The pitch and lack of echo tells me it is not the TV—someone's here.

After waiting another moment, I knock again. And again. Until whoever's inside creeps out towards the door.

Through the small frame of stained glass above it, I spy a redheaded woman. The glass distorts her features, but I can sense her apprehension from a mile away.

Even though she wasn't given a specific date or time, the IRS does alert people when they're going to be audited.

When it becomes obvious she's not going to open the door, I sigh. "Ma'am, are you going to let me in?"

She squeaks and crashes to the floor, and I wince in sympathy as her ankle twists underneath her.

"N-nobody's home!" she attempts, and I hang my head.

We're off to a great start.

"Listen, I promise that you have nothing to fear. I come in peace."

The woman clambers to her feet, muttering some more, and finally opens the door. I have my non-threatening smile pasted to my face, but it falls away as I drink in the vision before me.

Short red hair threaded with bands of gold frame the woman's heart-shaped face. Her large, hazel eyes are tinted both brown and green with flecks of yellow.

She's tall for a woman, but still would likely only come to my shoulders. Her form is thick and curvaceous, and my mouth waters.

In a word, the woman is stunning.

"Miss Fern Mabon?" I manage to ask past the lust hammering my body.

"Yes?"

"I'm Ahnou Napa with the IRS. I'd like to talk to you about your taxes."

From her dumbstruck expression, I can only surmise she had no clue that I was coming, or she had forgotten.

Miss Mabon blinks rapidly, as if in a daze, before asking me to join her. Then, the redheaded woman turns on her heel, leaving me no choice but to follow her inside.

The view of her ass covered in what looks like pajama bottoms does *nothing* to help the heat spreading through my limbs.

I remind myself that IRS employees don't check out the very rounded bottoms of their auditees as Miss Mabon walks into what I assume is her living room.

With a flick of her wrist, she gestures for me to sit down on an orange couch that's a few shades lighter and yellower than her hair.

The air feels charged with an inexplicable tension as our eyes lock. Fern's gaze holds a mixture of uncertainty and curiosity, her lips slightly parted as if she's about to say something.

I can't help but feel the pull between us, a magnetic force that defies explanation. The simple act of being in her presence stirs something within me, something that I've long kept buried.

The gorgeous woman tucks a strand of hair behind her ear, her fingers brushing against her skin in a gesture that's both unconscious and mesmerizing.

"You know, I never imagined that an IRS auditor would be, um, like *you*."

I lean in slightly, my voice a low hum. "And how did you imagine an IRS auditor to be?"

She meets my gaze, hers searching mine for something I'm not sure I can name. "Not as good looking."

A relieved smile tugs at my lips as red spreads across her face, but I'm glad she isn't put out by the fact that I'm a monster—and that she finds me attractive.

"Thank you. I don't think anyone has ever complimented me before when I've come to audit them."

"About that, Mr. Napa—"

"Please, call me Ahnou."

The request slips past my lips, and the tension in the room becomes palpable, almost suffocating in its intensity.

It's as if we're tiptoeing on the edge of a precipice, unsure of whether to take the plunge or step back, but whether she's experiencing the same emotions as me, I can't say.

"Then please call me Fern."

"Perhaps…if we're alone."

The words are out before I can take them back, but the lovely female doesn't blink. Instead, her eyes dilate and the scent of her arousal perfumes the air.

Down boy, I caution my body, which thrums with awareness.

Fern's fingers clench the fabric against her thigh, a nervous habit that I find oddly endearing. "So, um, *Ahnou,* what happens next?"

I lean in just a fraction closer, my voice a husky whisper. "Well, Miss Mabon, I'll review the information you've provided and ensure that everything is in order."

Her breath hitches, and I can see the effect my proximity is having on her. She's not the only one affected—my own heart is pounding a rhythm that matches the rapid beat of hers.

Before I can fully process the moment, Fern speaks again, her voice slightly shaky. "And you're *sure* my taxes haven't been filed recently?"

"I'm sure."

She twitches as if electrocuted. "Excuse me. I need to make a phone call. Please, enjoy your tea."

I grimace, but nod. A little distance between the two of us can't hurt considering I want to tackle her to the ground and cover the woman in my scent.

Whatever I'm feeling, I need to get it under control—now. Under no circumstances should I be experiencing such powerful lust for a human.

But if I didn't know any better, I would swear I'm going into rut.

Chapter Three

FERN

Up until this point, divorcing my ex has been the worst experience of my life.

The time it took, the numerous court proceedings, and the hurtful things he said about me—all recorded and filed for anyone to read.

But right now, with my mother on the phone and an Anubis government agent in my living room, I want the earth to open up and swallow me whole.

"What do you mean you haven't filed my taxes for two years?!"

Mom's voice morphs into whining. "Fern! That was a rough time for me, too!"

My jaw goes slack. "It was *my* divorce!"

"And Chet is like a son to me. I consider him family—and you tore it apart!"

It takes everything inside of me not to break down and cry. "Mom, he was hurting me. He said terrible things to me—don't you even care?"

She tuts on the other side of the line. "Honey, *everyone* says things that they regret and they don't mean it. People aren't perfect—that's why we have forgiveness. Unless you think you're above forgiveness?"

I fork a hand through the side of my hair, the clip holding it in place clacking against the phone, and I swear I can hear my mom cringe.

"Are you wearing that childish barrette again?"

"It's not a barrette, Mom, it's just a clip to keep my bangs out of my face."

"Well, it makes your hair look ridiculous. I don't know why you cut it so short after the divorce. Chet always loved it long." *That's exactly why I cut it.* "Are you listening to me, Fern Autumn? You're never going to win Chet back if you don't start looking presentable!"

Inhaling sharply, I count down from ten. "Mom, where's all the money that I set aside quarterly for taxes?"

The line goes silent. I pull back to make sure we haven't lost connection—or the more probable reason, that she hung up on me.

Nope.

Still connected.

"Mom?"

"Listen, honey, Chet needed help getting back on his feet—and who could blame him after the way that you took him through the wringer?"

My eye twitches. "You…gave my tax money to my *ex*?!"

"He's disabled! Fern, are you really so heartless?"

Glancing to see if my neighbors are looking, I kick and stomp the grass like the child my mother accuses me of being, but it's either this or I scream until my head explodes.

Finally, I get a hold of my temper. "Disabled? Really, Mom? He broke his toe *five* years ago—a week after we got married. They pinned it, and within a month and a half, he was fine. Heck, he was even cleared to get a job. I'm the one who's worked my butt off while he never, ever did anything!"

"Yes, well, I don't know if we consider it work, dear, when it's that wretched café of yours."

Great.

Today must be *'throw everything in Fern's face day'*.

"Speaking of the café, why aren't you at it?"

I pause. "Um, how do you know I'm not?"

"Because I passed it a bit ago, and your car wasn't there."

"I'm at home. I took the afternoon off. Seraphina is helping me."

"Are you sick?"

"What? No. I just wanted an afternoon to myself."

"Did you make four dozen cookies and eat them all?"

Red tints my cheeks. "No!"

It was only two dozen.

"You know, just because you work at a bakery doesn't mean you have to eat everything in it!"

To my mortification, tears fill my eyes and spill down my cheeks.

"Why are you so cruel?" I ask, my voice quivering. "Don't you even care that I could go to jail for tax evasion?"

"Please. Stop being so dramatic. I have some money that I can loan you."

My eyes bug at her announcement, and I'm uncertain which is more shocking—the fact that she is offering to loan me money or that she even has any saved.

Mom is a spender, while my father was a saver.

I rub my chest at the thought of my dad, the only person who ever truly believed in me. Maybe if he were still alive, I wouldn't have married Chet.

Where my dad was infinitely kind, my mom is the opposite—she doesn't do anything for free, even for her own daughter.

Hell, I'm convinced she treats strangers better than me.

"You're going to loan me money that I have to pay you back when you stole from me in the first place?"

"Don't talk to your mother like that! And I didn't steal anything. I appropriated it where it belonged. Since it's your *and* your husband's money, I was just giving it to another rightful owner."

"Mom, Chet and I aren't married—we're divorced."

"Not technically."

Well, shit sticks, she has a point. Two years ago, Chet and I separated. Until recently, we *were* still legally married.

"That still doesn't give you the right to misappropriate the money for the café!"

"I'm sorry. It slipped my mind."

Closing my eyes, I count backwards from ten.

"Right. Of course. I can see how something like this would "slip your mind.""

"Sarcasm is the witless woman's humor, Fern."

Note to self: make an appointment with the dentist to check that my back teeth aren't cracked from grinding them so hard.

"Apologies for my lack of comedic intellect. For this loan, what's your stipulation?"

"I will give you the money, and you won't have to pay me back, if…you get back together with Chet!"

Yep, definitely going to vomit.

Ahnou sits exactly where I left him, waiting for me. I wonder how tedious his job must be. "Sorry. I just got off the phone with my mom."

He waves my apology aside. "Are you alright?"

"Ugh…" I trail off, unsure of what he is asking specifically.

Am I alright in general?
About talking with my mom?
With being audited?
All three are a 'no'.

"I heard you in the bathroom. I, ah, don't mean to make you uncomfortable, but I have a keen sense of hearing."

"Oh my God—you heard me barfing?!" I blurt out without thinking, feeling even sicker.

The room begins to spin, and I'm sure that I'm about to embarrass myself more and pass out.

The next thing I know, Ahnou is at my side, guiding me gently to the couch. He presses me into the cushions before sitting beside me, his gaze fixed on my face.

"There's nothing to be ashamed of—it's a bodily function. I am more worried about you."

His kind words soothe my frayed nerves. "Nobody ever cares for me," I whisper, the statement slipping out before I can stop it.

Ahnou lets out a ferocious growl. "What do you mean nobody ever cares for you?"

His dark eyes narrow into slits, his tail rising and twitching with agitation.

Is he really this upset on my behalf?

"It's nothing! Never mind me."

He stares, clearly not believing a word I say but eventually grumbles and eases to the other side of the couch, giving me some space.

"How much do I owe the IRS?'

Ahnou leans over to pull out his briefcase once more, opening it and putting on the gold glasses that somehow make him even more endearing.

Something about the man makes me feel golden and fuzzy inside—until he reads the number on the paper.

And then I want to puke all over again.

The Anubis hums. "It's going to be ok. This is just what the IRS has calculated based on what they know from the numbers reported. It could be more—but it could be less depending on a multitude of things.”

“Less sounds promising. More sounds…” I trail off, feeling as if the Egyptian death gods themselves are punishing me. “Either way, I can get you the money. I just need to know the exact amount and the very latest I can send it in.”

“To do that, we need to file the past two years’ taxes. They both need to be approved by the IRS, and then we can set you up on a payment plan if needed.”

“A payment plan?”

Sweet buttery biscuits, maybe there’s hope for me after all.

“Yes, The IRS understands that some people don't have this amount of money to pay immediately, but there is a penalty that you incur—ten percent of what is owed that accrues over time.”

The hope that had blossomed inside my chest burst like a needle to a balloon.

Even if I somehow manage to owe less, that amount with the penalty added will take me forever to pay off—*and who's to say my mom even has that kind of money?*

When my dad died five years ago, he left me a nest egg knowing that my mom would never support me in my dream of opening a café, but he also set aside money for his wife.

Given my mom's opulent lifestyle, I really doubted she had anything left. I bet she was just saying that to get me to go back out with Chet.

I moan, my head dropping to my hands. This whole thing is a disaster that even a TV drama couldn't make up.

Hiccupping back my tears, I wallow in my misery. "I'm doomed."

Once more, Ahnou tips my chin up with a black claw. He brushes aside a piece of my red bangs that flop into my eye.

"Don't worry, Fern. We'll get through this together."

His sweet words and the tender way he touches me must be too much for my brain because something short circuits.

The next thing I know, a whimper echoes around us—*my whimper.*

And not one of pain or agony for the situation that I'm in.

No.

One of need.

Chapter Four

AHNOU

Remain impartial.

It's the number one rule of the IRS, and up until this point, it's never been an issue for me, but when Fern lets out the neediest sound I've ever heard, all professionalism flies out the window.

She smells like sunshine, flowers—and slick.

My mouth waters, wanting a taste. Before I can think, the dormant alpha inside of me reacts, pulling Fern into my lap,

I thought I'd tamped back the greedy, asshole side of myself a long time ago.

It has no place in human society. Whether monsters liked it or not, we have to conform to the human world.

For me, it's been easy. Anubis males go into rut only when near a female who's in heat, but working for the IRS and traveling as much as I do has pretty much cut me off from my kind.

Over time, I slipped into my introverted, studious side, all but ignoring the animal that lurks in all my kind.

What baffles me is why Fern is eliciting such a reaction from me. Humans, to the best of my knowledge, don't have cycles like Anubis do.

But one, deep inhale tells me that the female in my lap is experiencing some kind of heat—*and it's throwing me into a rut.*

The practical side of me screams to push Miss Mabon off my lap, but the logic is drowned out by the arousal Fern evokes inside of me.

Reaching down, I grasp the twin globes of her ass, grinding her form into mine. She shudders, reaching forward to brace herself on my shoulders, her hazel eyes wide.

The greenish-brown orbs are flecked with gold that nearly matches the highlights in her red hair.

Her eyes shutter closed as I flex her hips forward and circle her pussy over the crotch of my suddenly too-tight slacks.

She mewls, the erotic noise transforming into low moans as our movements pick up speed.

In the darkest recesses of my mind, I acknowledge that dry humping a client is the lowest of lows.

It guarantees my termination from the IRS, but I couldn't stop myself if I tried. Especially when Fern bites her lips and cries out.

"Oh, fuck! Ahnou, please don't stop!"

Baring my teeth, I hiss at the delicious friction building between the two of us. Fern leans in even closer, her large breasts brushing against the lapels of my suit as she blindly reaches for my snout, tipping it downward.

And I receive my first kiss.

I'd seen the human display of affection from time to time, but my secret fetish for them maybe meant I had a completely separate phone stashed with human porn focused on the art of locking lips.

Hers are softer than Maat's feather, whispering across the dark line of my mouth, followed by the kitten-like flick of her tongue.

The woman is more tempting than Bast herself, and my khenen pushes against the zipper of my slacks painfully.

My keen hearing picks up on the sound of the steel ball pierced through the tip brushing against the metal of my zipper.

Fern's body shudders against mine, and I echo the movement, both of us desperate for release.

I try to return her kiss, but I feel inept and worry that she might think I'm a clumsy oaf. Pulling back, I lick along her jawline when I realize that I'm panting like a dog that humans so often liken us to.

An apology forms on my tongue for my embarrassing behavior when Fern reopens her eyes, the greenish-brown hue nearly indiscernible.

The black of her pupils is blown wide, and I realize she's breathing just as heavily as I am.

"Please—I'm so close."

Unable to resist her plea, I bounce her up and down the hard, ridged outline of my khenen.

Fern's head falls back, exposing the long, delicate line of her neck, and I bury my muzzle into it.

Unconsciously, I skim the sharp edges of my canines along her sensitive flesh, unable to help myself.

Need, fiery and hot, spirals down my spine, and my knot pulses with desperation to fill the female before me.

I want to lock the two of us in place until Fern's body overflows with my cum, but even I won't cross that line. My khenen vibrates, and I know I'm close to coming.

Out of nowhere, I growl, "Tell me I'm a good boy."

The redheaded darling in my arms doesn't even miss a beat. "Ah, you're such a good, good boy, making me so wet—"

My canines snap, sinking into the delicate layers of her skin. As Fern goes rigid in my arms, she lets out a scream that nearly pierces my eardrum, convulsing hard in my lap as she comes from my bite.

And that's all it takes to tip me over the edge.

My khenen jerks forward as jet after jet of cum soaks the inside of my slacks. The thick, creamy liquid pools around my knot, offering it no relief.

It's swollen and hard, and my thighs shake with the desperation I feel at not being inside of Fern.

Since I'm not locked with a female, it'll only take minutes for the swelling to subside—just enough time for both Fern and me to gather our bearings.

And remember who we are.

My onyx fur doesn't display my embarrassment as boldly as Fern's skin does, but I understand the sentiment.

"I'm so so sorry, Fern. I mean, Miss Mabon. I don't know what came over me."

She stares at me with large, hazel eyes, perhaps too shell-shocked to speak. When I try to pick her up, she wraps her long legs around my waist.

"You made me come."

It's a statement, but laced with wonder.

"Well, I don't know if I can take all the credit. We both kind of lost our heads there for a moment."

"Did…did you come?"

I grimace, knowing men didn't come in their pants, but for some reason, I wouldn't lie to her.

"Yes."

Fern whimpers.

Another. Fucking. Whimper.

And I swear to all the death gods in the world, I'm hard again.

Her blush intensifies, creeping down her face and below the collar of her oversized sweater.

Would her tits flush the same gorgeous red as her face?

What about her ass if I smacked it while fucking her from behind?

And I've officially crossed and recrossed the line.

"No one's ever made me…you know."

Fern's soft words pull my head out of my mental crisis. I mull them over before her meaning dawns.

"Are you telling me that no one's ever made you come before?"

She shakes her head.

I bite my lip, wanting to ask more, but unsure of whether it's too personal or not.

Fuck it, Ahnou, you've not only crossed all the lines but erased them, too.

"Have you never been intimate with another person?"

The idea makes the possessive beast inside of me howl in victory, until she answers.

"Yes. I was married up until recently, although my ex and I had been separated for over two years."

My eyes narrow at the thought of someone else touching the delectable morsel in my lap. "And why wasn't *he* making you come?"

Jealousy wars with logic. Obviously, there's no reason to be envious of her ex. Not only is he no longer with Fern, but it was before me.

And that's what I hate—that there were others before me.

That's the rut talking, Ahnou!

But I shouldn't be in a rut, not because of a human. Maybe a female Anubis is nearby and triggered my need, but I ended up imprinting upon Fern.

It's a long shot, but the only thing my mind can come up with that's rational—not that I'm being particularly logical.

Fern shrugs. "I don't think my pleasure was ever his concern—just his."

Another snarl bursts past my lips. "What a jackass. Sorry for using such language in the presence of a lady, but I'm glad you divorced him. You're a rare and sparkling gem, Fern, never forget that."

She giggles, which only makes my chest squeeze tighter. "I don't think anyone would call me a lady right now…"

Although I know she's teasing, her words upset me. "Ladies are allowed pleasure. I was raised that all women are ladies, and not in the way that puts societal restrictions on the term.

Rather, one where men show women respect—you are the backbone of society and that position demands everyone's highest regard."

Fern gapes, her mouth literally dropped open, displaying the small pink expanse of her tongue.

Can I get any harder?

"Where have you been all my life?"

She whispers the words, seemingly unaware that she even spoke, and my chest swells with happiness at the wonder I've given her.

But before I can do or say anything, there's a knock on the door, abruptly dispelling whatever erotic enchantment that's woven around us.

If I thought coming in my pants was awkward, it's nothing compared to what lies ahead.

Chapter Five

FERN

My mom, my ex, and a monstrous tax auditor all walk onto my porch…

There is no punch line, but I'm pretty for sure the universe thinks my life is a joke or else I wouldn't be standing here in pajama pants soaked with my own arousal for everyone to see.

"Did you pee your pants?"

Of course, Chet would look at my crotch first and blurt out the most embarrassing thing that comes to his mind.

"Oh my God, Fern! You're almost forty—" *In nine years.* "—what is going on with you?!" Mom hisses.

"I didn't pee my pants!"

It's a lame defense since a) my pajamas are pastel colored and there's a giant, dark stain where the legs meet and b) the truth can never be told.

Mom sniffs, clearly not convinced. "I think you need someone to take care of you."

Cripes, you pseudo-piss your pants one time, and suddenly, you can't take of yourself.

"Listen, this is all a big misunderstanding— not that it's anyone's business. Mom, can you come back later *without* Chet, please?"

"Chet's going to stay here. I'm worried about leaving you alone."

"No, Chet's *not* going to stay here. He's not welcome in my home."

"That's no way to treat your husband!"

"Are you insane?! We're divorced!"

"That can be fixed," my mother mutters. "I'll go get a minister and some Depends."

Throughout this hellish conversation, Ahnou has remained quiet, but now, a growl rumbles in his chest.

"It's *slick*," he snarls with such ferocity that we all take a step back.

"Come again?" Mom says, finally acknowledging the Anubis.

She isn't particularly fond of monsters for some reason. Knowing her, she probably thinks humans are better—a foolish outlook when you consider the scope of human crime.

"That's exactly what happened. Fern came—again and again. It's *not* urine staining her pants. It's *slick*."

I never knew silence could be so deafening.

My mother slits her eyes. "Are you the auditor?"

He opens his mouth to, likely, tell her the truth, and for some reason, I can't let Ahnou take the fall.

What happened between us was beyond both our control. I have no way to explain how or why, but every instinct inside of me rises to defend the man I just met.

"He's my boyfriend."

The words are out before I can take them back. As expected, Mom flies into a fit while Chet stomps his foot like a child denied their favorite toy.

Before either of them can start their tantrum, Ahnou wraps a giant paw around my waist and yanks me back through the door, slamming it shut in their shocked faces.

He throws the bolt in place, ensuring that even if my mom brought her spare key, she won't be able to get in.

After my divorce, I changed all the locks since Chet had a nasty habit of showing up unannounced.

With a sinking feeling, I realize my mom probably already gave him a copy of the spare key.

Now I'll have to get new locks.

Ahnou steps back to give me some space while I listen to my mom screech on the other side of the door.

As if realizing she's not going to stop any time soon, the Anubis takes my hand and drags me into my living room.

"I'm sorry," I whisper, sick to my core that he had to witness that.

He blinks his large golden eyes. "What are you apologizing for?"

"My mom, Chet, and…for what happened before." I point between our two bodies, unable to look up at him.

"That's a dangerous habit," he rumbles.

"What is?"

"Apologizing for others. You don't control another adult's actions, and you clearly have disassociated yourself with them—so why should you be taking the responsibility of what they say or do?"

On the one hand, he's right. I'm not holding a gun to my mom's or Chet's head, and I *definitely* separated myself from Chet by divorcing him.

My mom is a different kettle of fish altogether, though.

If not for my father's dying wishes, she and I might not have our strained relationship at all, but Dad asked me to be the bigger person.

The two of us are all we have left, and some days it seems petty to want to turn my back on that. On other days—like today—she's lucky I gave my father my vow.

"As for what happened between *us*," Ahnou growls, snapping my attention back to him. "*I* should be the one to apologize—it was unprofessional and out of line. I don't know what came over me. It's like I couldn't…"

"Couldn't control yourself," I finish for him.

He nods, and although neither of us say it, I know both of us felt the same way, like there was an invisible string tying a cord around us, pulling us closer and closer until we had no choice but to crash into one another.

"Why did you tell your mom that I'm your boyfriend?"

My skin flushes. "I didn't want you to get in trouble. If she knew you were the auditor, she'd call the IRS and you'd be fired."

Ahnou swipes a paw along his muzzle, one black claw clanking against the sharp white of his canine.

The sight of it reminds me of his teeth on my neck, and I raise a hand to touch the mark. His gaze flashes down and his expression twists.

"I *should* be fired for what I did—I've marked you, Fern."

Without a mirror, I can only conjure the image of the hickey blooming on the tender skin of my throat in my mind's eye.

I wave his concern away with a laugh, though it's more forced than genuine. "I bruise easily, like a peach. It's not a big deal. In a few days, it'll fade."

The Anubis fidgets, his foot scuffing the rug in my living room. His voice, deep and low, barely reaches my ears as he murmurs, "No, it won't."

I frown, perplexed. "What do you mean?"

He meets my gaze, his eyes filled with an intensity that makes my heart race. "The mark of an Anubis on their mate is permanent."

His words hang in the air, heavy with meaning that my brain hesitates to fully comprehend.

My brows knit together. "Forgive me," I say, my voice tinged with unease. "I don't know much about...monsters. My mother has never been fond of them, and I've grown up rather ignorant."

Ahnou offers a sympathetic smile. "I understand. I've tried to educate myself as I grew older, but there are so many different kinds, each of us unique."

"Well, I don't know anything about the Anubis species, but surely biting my neck doesn't bond us together as you're suggesting."

The towering giant lets out a sigh, running a dark hand between his ears and down the back of his head.

"It's the first step when a male Anubis is thrown into a rut. He can choose to slake his lust without marking a female. But I've avoided one so long that my body took over for me. It wants a mate—and it's chosen you."

"A rut?" I repeat, ignoring the terrifying part at the end of his statement.

"Yes. When a female Anubis goes into heat, it triggers a rut or a mating frenzy in the nearest males."

I shake my head, disbelieving. "But I couldn't have thrown you into a rut. I'm human, after all!"

Ahnou rubs his temple, a sign of his own frustration. "I didn't think humans went into heat, either. There must be a female Anubis nearby who is invoking such...lust."

The notion sends a shiver down my spine—and not a good one. The idea of another woman, monster or not, stirring such desires in a man I've known for only an hour unsettles me.

The covetousness that creeps into my thoughts surprises me—I've never been possessive in my life.

Warning bells clang in my head, but I push them aside. "So claiming someone as a mate involves more than just biting their neck?"

"Well, the mark needs to be reinforced during intercourse, and then a male Anubis needs to brand his mate with his seed."

The visions he invokes leaves me momentarily speechless, my denial caught in my throat.

An image of me, bare and exposed, beneath his large form and coated in his cum, etches itself forever in my mind. It's both arousing and frightening, and my cheeks flush with heat.

"What are you thinking about, Fern?"

"Nothing naughty," I reply too quickly, though my attempt at nonchalance is in vain.

His dark chuckle resonates in the room, carrying an undertone of desire.

"If need wasn't clouding your voice and coloring your cheeks, I'd still know you were lying—I can smell you, kianga."

The admission surprises me, as does the term of endearment, and a squeak escapes my lips. "Smell me?!"

He leans closer, his unwavering golden gaze locked onto mine. "Mmhmm. And you smell like the forbidden ambrosial nectar of the gods."

The intensity in his words sets my nerves ablaze. Desire curls low in my belly, a yearning I've never experienced before.

The room heats up, the temperature rising to an inferno, threatening to consume us both. I'm a heartbeat away from shedding my clothes and surrendering to the fire that burns between us.

"Do I need to get a lawyer?" I manage to ask, my voice strained with the effort to remain coherent.

Ahnou's gaze darkens with amusement, his lips tugging into a grin as if he knows my every thought. "For what?"

"My taxes!"

"No, I meant what I said. I'll help you get everything set to rights.

"And how long will that take?"

His smile grows even wider. "For as long as it takes."

This leaves me unsettled, a feeling I despise, since I'm a control freak in everything but one area of my life.

"Um, ok, do I give you my information, and then you go back to the IRS, er, headquarters?"

Ahnou chuckles. "Headquarters? The IRS isn't a villainous government entity. But no, I won't be going anywhere. I'll be staying here in Cedar Peak Heights."

I scratch at my neck and arms, my discomfort growing. "But this town is so small. It's inevitable that we'll run into each other."

"Fern, there's no escaping me—not to mention you told your mother and ex that we're dating." *Oh, right.* "Besides, you need my help in more areas of your life than just taxes."

"I do?"

"Yep."

"And what exactly will you be helping me with?

The Anubis leans in, his eyes holding a hint of mischief.

"Getting payback."

"P-payback? How?"

"Come on a date with me and find out."

"A date? Like a real one?! I'm not sure—"

"I'll make you come again, even harder."

Shit, why didn't he lead with that?

Chapter

Six

AHNOU

Despite the lore of my kind's origins, I'm not a particularly vengeful creature. Even so, every instinct inside of me screams to humiliate Fern's mother and her ex-mate.

Both repulse me, yet not as much as her mother.

To Anubis, offspring are sacred—a privilege, not a right. A parent's role is to nurture their cub into their happiest self.

Fern's mother can't see past herself, and it's etched scars deep into her daughter, not that the redheaded wonder shows it.

She's a queen, holding her head high and exuding sunshine from her soul. I want to bottle it up and carry it around with me forever.

I don't understand her contentment but know I want to bask in it forever—which is why I marked her.

It wasn't intentional, but I also wasn't honest with Fern. She thinks mating with me can still be avoided, but it can't.

At least, not on my end.

When an Anubis male picks a mate and marks her, he imparts a piece of himself onto her. Imprinting is just part of the process that bonds mates together.

If I stop now, the mark on Fern's neck will only itch occasionally, especially if I'm nearby. As a human, I don't think it will affect her as strongly.

She'll be able to live her life with the freedom she deserves—especially after being married to someone like Chet.

But me, on the other hand, will forever be tethered to the beautiful redhead that somehow managed to steal my heart in less than sixty minutes.

To be without Fern is to be miserable, but I deserve no less for marking her without her consent.

It was a deeply ingrained, subconscious act on my part, but it still doesn't negate what I did, and I would never force anyone into a partnership with me.

Logically, the smart thing to do right now would be to call the IRS head office and request a transfer, but I'm not leaving Fern's future in the hands of another auditor.

Something's going on in her life, and I'm going to figure it out and help her finally break free of her mother and her ex-husband.

By the time I drive away from Cedar Peak Heights, Fern will know her worth. I'll be damned if she doesn't act like the goddess she is.

Starting by promising her more orgasms.

Inwardly, I groan, because I shouldn't be bribing an auditee with pleasure. When this job is done, I definitely will need to resign from the IRS.

That is, if they don't fire me first.

But then I can move back to Egypt to be with my kind, maybe even get a job with my cousin, guarding the ancient temples of Karnak.

My mouth curves into a frown. The idea sounds even more abysmal than my current job, partly because I enjoy working with numbers, but mostly because I don't want to leave Fern.

She's still staring at me with owlishly large eyes.

"P-payback?" she stammers, her cheeks redder than the madder roots my ancestors used to dye cloth.

The woman is too adorable, focusing on my promise of payback instead of giving her pleasure, and it takes all my will not to yank her back into my arms because she smells like she wants to come again.

"Trust me," I soothe.

Run away while you can.

She shifts, rubbing her hands over the tops of her thighs as if she can hear my thoughts, but she doesn't flee.

Instead, Fern leans in closer, her tongue flicking out to lick her full lower lip. My gut clenches at the sight, as further south hardens.

"Okay, I trust you."

I pick up my briefcase to stand, and my claws shred the underside of the buttery leather because I'm clenching it so hard to keep from touching the vision before me.

"Excellent. For now, I will depart. I need to find a place to stay and report back to my head office.

No one besides us has to know that I'm here to audit you. For all intents and purposes, I'm your boyfriend—I'll make sure your ex doesn't bother you while I'm here."

Fern stares up at me, her lower lip trembling. "Thank you."

Gripping my briefcase harder, I take a deep breath and remind myself that if I reach out to stroke her cheek, I'll likely end up stroking something else.

And I've already crossed enough lines.

My poor briefcase trembles under the brutality of my claws. When this is done, I'm going to need a new one.

The lovely redhead walks me to her door, peeking out to make sure everyone is gone before opening it.

"Do you want to meet me for dinner?"

Fern squirms. "It's kind of a small town…"

I chuckle at her reiteration. "And?"

"Everyone will see us together!"

"That's kind of the point—unless you don't want to be seen with me…"

She rolls her eyes. "It's not you. It's *me.* Everyone knows me and talks."

I crouch down until I'm at eye level with her. "Tune them out. Their gossip isn't your truth."

A brilliant smile spreads across her face, and she lunges forward, wrapping her arms around my neck to give me a hug.

I hold my breath, not daring to move a muscle, never wanting this moment to end, but it does when Fern eventually pulls back.

"How about we meet at the diner—the only one in town on the corner of Main Street. Say at six?"

"Sounds like a date," I whisper.

Hastily, I leave before I can lose my self-control.

Again.

My heart pounds as I turn to walk away, each step feeling like a reluctant retreat. Even with my back to her, I sense Fern's very essence.

Like a magnetic pull that threatens to yank me back to her side, my body fights against my brain to turn and go back to her.

"See you in a bit!" I toss over my shoulder, my voice laced with unchecked passion.

Fuck, get it together.

As I walk away, I draw in a deep breath of the crisp autumn air, trying to steady the rapid rhythm of my heartbeat.

I shake my head as I cram into my tiny car. Entangling myself with Fern wasn't part of the plan, yet I can't deny the electricity that surges between us.

It's like we have this connection that defies reason, and I'm torn between respecting the woman I just met by giving her space or spending every waking moment with her until she realizes we were meant to be.

Psycho monster alert—even I think my thoughts sound unhinged.

Trying to push Fern from my head, I drive down the block and spy a house for rent. It's a lovely, old Victorian that's seen better days.

Traditionally, the IRS would prefer I pick a hotel, but given that I'm going to be here for a bit, I decide to call the number listed on the sign in front of the house.

A woman answers after the first ring. "Hello?"

"Hi, I'm calling about the house for rent on the corner of Maple Crest and Pine Dale. Is it still available?"

"Yes, it certainly is."

"Do you do contracts for short term? A month, two months max?"

"Since I have no current interest in the place, I have no problem with this."

"Excellent. If you would like to get the contract drawn up, I can come sign it and send you the funds for one month and a retainer for the second, just in case."

"No need for a contract! I live next door. It was my sister's house before she passed. Why don't you stop by so I can meet you and give you the key?"

Although I'm not comfortable working without a contract, I decide not to push the issue over the phone.

"Of course. I'm in front of the house now, so I'll be right over."

I park in the driveway next to the Victorian just as an elderly woman hobbles down the front steps.

At the last second, her cane catches on some loose wood and she tumbles forward, losing her balance.

Before she can scream, I'm before her. She blinks in confusion as I gently set her upright and on the sidewalk.

"Oh my…that was close. Thank you, young man."

This elicits a chuckle from me. "I'm not that young anymore."

The woman adjusts her glasses, staring up at me. "Younger than me, sonny!"

"You've got me there. I'm Ahnou Napa, nice to meet you. I'm the one who called about renting the house."

"Well met, Mr. Napa. I'm Francine, and thank you for catching me. If I take one more tumble, my son and daughter-in-law are going to put me in a retirement home."

Francine tuts in disgust, and I swallow all the laughter threatening to come out.

"I just happened to be in the right place at the right time."

"Can't say I've ever seen anyone move so fast. You're like a veritable superhero, Mr. Napa. My great grandson would go ga-ga over you."

"It was nothing. Anubis are naturally agile. Again, I'm thankful I was there in time."

"Are other Anubis as muscular and handsome?"

Now, I shift, ducking my head. "We're all built similarly, ma'am. Nothing special, just your typical death god monsters."

She smirks. "Handsome and humble, what a delightful combination. Tell me—are you single?" Francine cackles at what I assume is my horrified expression. "Not for me, sonny, for my great niece."

"Um, I'm afraid not, actually."

"Pity. You would've been perfect for my Sera—the death to her life, if you will. So what brings you to Cedar Peak Heights?"

"Work. It's why I asked for a contract, as my boss will need to see a financial receipt."

"Ah, I see. Ok, I'll figure something out. You said a month or two?"

"I'll do two, just in case."

"Lovely. Let me find the key." Francine turns and ambles back up the steps of her porch. "Who do you work for?"

Even though I know she's just making small talk, I don't want to say for Fern's sake. "Actually, I'm not at liberty to say."

This brings the older woman up short. "Are you a spy?!" My mouth drops open in shock as I try to get the words out denying the accusation, but Francine just cackles. "Don't worry—your secret is safe with me! Ooo, boy, these next sixty days are going to be interesting! It's been a while since this town has seen anything to shake it up."

I grimace.

This is exactly what I'm afraid of.

Chapter Seven

FERN

I rush into my café like my butt's on fire. Only a handful of regulars occupy the space, and they all stop what they're doing to stare at me.

"Sorry, everyone, you'll have to leave—family emergency."

More like a business emergency that's devolved into a personal one…

I'll make you come again, even harder.

Ahnou's promise rings in my ears louder than the music in the front row of a rock concert.

My best—and only—friend, Serafina, pins her icy stare on me, her eyes wide. "What's the matter? Did Chet finally take a short walk off a long cliff?"

Her last question carries a glimmer of desperate hope that makes me chuckle. "No, but it's related to something like death. Sort of. I'm being audited…by an Anubis. Oh, and we've got a date."

Serafina's white brows shoot up, nearly blending with her hairline. "Isn't that a conflict of interest?"

"It's complicated."

"Sounds like it. Tell me everything and don't leave any details out."

Yikes.

With resignation, I launch into the full story, beginning with the harsh reality of my tax woes and ending with me awkwardly entangled with my auditor.

The only thing I leave out is my mom's involvement. Sera and she do *not* get along at all, and I don't want to add fuel to that fire.

My bestie's expression transforms into pure shock. "I can't believe you let a stranger touch you!"

I blush, knowing Sera isn't chastising my actions, just that I've erected so many barriers over the last two years.

Not to mention the ones that were already in place…hiding a shameful secret I've concealed since childhood.

Even though I trust Seraphina explicitly, revealing the truth isn't an option. Only my mom knows, and she pretends that she doesn't.

Serafina squints, her stare boring into me before her shoulders relax. "Sorry, that sounded bad. You know I'm not here to judge.

Besides, I think this guy might be exactly what you need to put your mom and Chet in their place. And if he can assist with your taxes and get you off, that's a win-win."

"So you think I should keep up the charade of Ahnou being my boyfriend?"

"Well, I definitely think you should make the most of this situation and milk it for all it's worth— and I mean that in the filthiest way possible."

I laugh so hard when Seraphina waggles her eyebrows that I have to clamp a hand over my boobs to keep them from jiggling in the most embarrassing way.

"How can you look like an angel but think like the devil?" She winces, and I wonder if I hit a nerve. "Everything ok?"

"Yeah, it's nothing. How about we get you all dolled up for your date?"

The look on her face says it's *something*, but Sera never pries and always supports me and she deserves the same from me.

"Ok, work your magic, but don't be too upset if you don't get the results you want. You can't turn a warty gourd into a perfect pumpkin."

Seraphina rolls her eyes, used to my self-deprecating humor. She ushers me toward the rear of the café, where a set of stairs leads to an apartment that she lives in up above.

It was part of the building's package, and back then, I had no intentions of using it— maybe for extra storage—but then, like a serendipitous twist, Serafina entered my life.

She helped to patch up my broken pieces when I needed it most, and I wanted to repay the kindness by providing her a place to stay.

Together, we march into Sera's bedroom, which is a chaotic mess of clothing, a sharp contrast to how clean the rest of the place is.

"Ok, I've got something in mind for you—"

I snort, cutting her off. Although Serafina and I stand at nearly the same height, I outweigh her by a landslide.

If, by some magic, I managed to shoehorn myself into her clothing, the seams would burst faster than a balloon bounced around a cage full of porcupines.

"Not gonna happen, Sera."

"You're not going to pop through the seams of my clothes."

"Are you reading my thoughts?"

Seraphina blushes, the soft pink a gorgeous flush over her dark skin, and I try not to be envious of how lovely it looks on her.

When I blush, I look like an angry man who's about to have a hernia.

"Listen, your mom's voice isn't your own. I've heard her words often enough to know the poison she feeds you, and it's not right, Fern.

You're not fat, and you're not ugly. You're absolutely stunning, inside and out. I know it's hard to hear this, but your mom is…not a good person. She's just masking her cruelty as concern."

A frown forms on my lips because I know Sera's right, but I can't help but defend the woman who gave birth to me. "My mom is hard on me because she loves me."

"No, Fern. If your mother said those things to anyone else, would you find it acceptable? If she called me 'fat', would that be ok?"

"No, definitely not!"

"Then why is it alright for her to say it to *you*?"

Serafina's question lingers in the air. I understand her point, but how do I explain my sense of obligation without sounding like a nut job?

"It's not right, but she's my mom…"

"You deserve happiness. You deserve to feel good about yourself and to be treated with dignity and respect. More actually—you deserve to be treated like a queen.

How many people are as kind as you? It pisses me off that your mom uses your greatest strength against you because you're one in a million."

The sincerity in her words tugs at my heartstrings, plucking a melancholic chord within that makes me realize how unhappy I still am.

But not when I was with Ahnou.

When we were together, I felt like a completely different person—alive, free, and connected.

Even though we had just met, it was obvious there was something between us, something Ahnou wants to explore further.

But only if that's what I want...*and I think I do.*

For the first time in a while, a flicker of hope ignites within my chest, casting a faint glow against the darkness of my relentless self-doubt.

Maybe, just maybe, being audited isn't the end of the world.

As Sera rummages in her closet, I kick around the idea of being Ahnou's mate, wondering what that would entail and why I find it so appealing after just finalizing my divorce.

After a few minutes, my friend turns around with a flourish to present me with a dress dyed blue like the midnight sky.

It's elegant yet not overly formal—the perfect blend of sophistication and comfort for a local date night with your government monster.

"What are you thinking?"

"That I've lost my mind. Oh, and that this will never fit no matter how stretchy the material feels."

Seraphina grunts. "Will you please just trust me? It's going to look amazing on you. Go try it on."

"Ok, I trust you."

Taking the dress, I retreat to the bathroom, staring at the gorgeous blue fabric with trepidation.

I send a quick prayer to the gods—who've never listened to me before—that I don't need medical attention to get this thing removed.

And then I slip it on.

Holy stromboli, Sera was right.

The little number somehow hugs me in all the right places, emphasizing my curves instead of my rolls.

Apparently, my bestie isn't just graced with inhuman beauty, but also possesses an innate understanding of fashion that I can only envy.

Maybe I should let Sera dress me all the time…

When I finally step out of the bathroom, she gasps. "I knew you would look phenomenal, but damn girl, you're a veritable goddess in that! I almost feel bad for your date."

I smirk at her antics. "And why would you feel bad for him?"

"Because he's going to have the biggest boner in public when he gets a glance at you!"

Now I cackle, the thought of the towering Anubis rocking a hard-on for everyone to see cracking me up, but my laughter quickly dries up as other parts of my body perk up at the image.

Just thinking of the man makes me wet.

Seraphina distracts me by taking my hand and leading me to stand before her full-length mirror. My reflection stares back, and I'm like a woman transformed.

A spark of something unfamiliar smolders beneath my skin, an ember of confidence I've been lacking.

For the first time in my life, I feel sexy.

"Am I right, or am I right—you looking uh-may-zing!" Sera crows.

Putting myself in her shoes, I glimpse a version of myself I've never beheld, and I wonder if this is what Ahnou sees when he looks at me.

"Thank you, Seraphina. I look nice."

She snorts. "No, you're fucking gorgeous. Say it."

"I'm fucking gorgeous."

"Louder!"

"I'M FUCKING GORGEOUS!" I scream at the top of my lungs and nearly collapse in a fit of giggles at the shocked expression on Sera's face. "You didn't expect me to do it, eh?"

"Not that loud or with that much conviction, but I should know better. No one's stronger than you, Fern."

Now I snort. "Please stop acting like I'm some rock star."

"But you are! You just don't know it yet, but you will."

"And why's that?"

"I have a feeling your Anubis is going to show you."

"He's not *my* Anubis," I mutter, blushing.

"Sounds like he could be if you wanted…"

"If you saw him, you would get it. I'm a thousand times out of his league."

Seraphina tsks as her hand, warm and steady, lands on my arm. It's like a physical anchor against the tide of my insecurities.

"Babe, you are *more* than in his league," she insists, her voice a beacon of unwavering support. "Just because Chet made you feel like you're not worthy doesn't mean you aren't. You just need to find a guy who sees how amazing you really are."

Her wisdom finds a home within me, settling in the corners of my heart. I nod, determined to carry Sera's inner strength with me on my first date in nearly a decade.

"You're right. Chet's damned words like to haunt my mind, but it's time to let that go. It's funny how I cut the physical cord with him but can't quite sever the mental one."

"They always say the deepest wounds are the ones you can't see. Don't beat yourself up. It's going to take time to completely get over the hurtful things Chet said and did.

And I think Ahnou is a great way to continue the healing process. Orgasms are like miracle workers, I swear. Get him to give you as many as he can—Dr. Sera's orders."

"When did you get your medical degree?"

"I was born with a PhD in Sexual Gratification."

Our gazes lock in the mirror as we bust up laughing. "That…is disturbing. What would I do without you?"

"Not get my excellent sex advice, that's what. Come on, let's find some shoes, and I'll curl your hair. It's so cute. I could never pull off a bob."

Rolling my eyes, I follow Sera back into the bathroom. I'm one hundred percent certain there isn't anything the woman couldn't pull off, even if she was dressed in plastic bags.

Twenty minutes later, I'm as ready as I'll ever be—physically, speaking. Seraphina worked her magic on my face and hair, but internally, I'm a bundle of nerves.

My best friend pulls me in for a hug, her embrace a sanctuary of comfort. "You've got this."

"I'm scared," I confess with a horrifying wobble to my voice.

Sera spins me so we're face-to-face. "New things can be scary, but mostly because you're projecting your past fears on them.

You're afraid Ahnou will be like Chet, but that's not fair to him or you. Give him a true chance—you deserve it. Tonight might mark the beginning of something incredible."

"Are you sure you don't have a degree in broken hearts?"

She winks. "I do."

Giggling, I shake my head and grab my purse. "Ok, I can do this."

"That's the spirit! Fern's getting laid!"

"Whoa! Laid?! I thought I was just after orgasms."

"Yeah, but the best ones are when you're stuffed with monster cock."

"Is this something you know from personal experience?"

Seraphina blushes—again—twice in one evening! "I'm not answering that. Now go!"

Part of me wants to pry out her secrets, but I won't, not when I won't share my own. "Fine, but someday, I want you to tell me!"

"Deal. Have fun tonight."

I turn back and give her a fierce hug. "I love you, Sera."

"Shit, don't make me cry. You know I'm a big baby! I love you, too, Fern."

Getting into my car, I wave good-bye one last time and drive away. In my rearview mirror, Seraphina stands, her long, white hair whipping like a flag in the wind.

The sight of her is a reminder that I'm not alone, no matter how awful my mom and Chet have made me feel. I have a true friend in this world, and maybe I've found another in Ahnou.

As I make my way closer to the diner, my heart beats a frenetic rhythm, a symphony of anxiety and anticipation.

The unknown lies ahead like an uncharted sea, waves of nervousness crashing against the shore of my resolve, but Sera's words ring in my head.

I need to give tonight a fair shot—not only for me, but also Ahnou.

Chapter
Eight
AHNOU

As people filter into the tiny diner for supper, they stare at me. To them, I'm a creature larger than life, or at least, far too large for the booth I'm wedged into.

They whisper, point, and are appallingly obvious, but their curiosity doesn't bother me. Unlike others I've encountered, there's no malice behind it.

I'm just a monster in a mostly human town.

At least, that's what I gathered when I went out this afternoon after leaving Fern's house and exploring Cedar Peak Heights a bit.

So I expect that while I'm here, I'll get more than a few long glances and a question or two, if anyone's brave enough.

There's a lot of mystery surrounding my kind, mostly about death and a secret, mystical power we supposedly hold, but it's not true.

We don't have any sway over who lives and dies. That actually belongs to another set of monsters.

And, for sure, if I had some kind of magic, I definitely wouldn't be working for the IRS.

Of course, even if I told this to people, it wouldn't stop anyone from spreading rumors. Truth be told, I'm probably the most exciting thing Cedar Peak Heights has seen in a long time.

Places like this thrive off gossip and scandal, mostly because, I assume, not much else happens. I'm happy to feed the former, but I'd prefer to stay away from the latter.

My boss made it clear that they don't like the US government entangled in drama, even though it creates quite a few scandals of its own.

The question is where's this line for Fern and me?

Where she's concerned, I want to do every scandalous thing running through my head. As if I summoned her with my naughty thoughts, she appears in the doorway of the diner.

The woman is a stunning vision—like a sacrificial offering to the ancient gods. If only I were the one she was being offered to.

Maat's feather, *I* would gladly give myself as an offering to her just to worship at her temple like the goddess she is, and I can't decide which I prefer more.

The duality inside of me fights, my alpha side, as usual with Fern, rising to the top as I envision her spread on an altar for me to do with as I please.

Damned alpha instincts nearly have me getting up to tackle the woman out the door to have my wicked way with her.

Down boy.

My inner alpha snarls but quiets down eventually, knowing what we want isn't how we should act, and I try to quell the whirlwind of emotions bombarding me.

Physically, I'm the embodiment of a leader. Anubis are born into a hierarchy that dictates their sexual orientation and makeup—but not necessarily our proclivities in bed.

The knot and ridges on my khenen told my parents at birth where I stood in this hierarchy. The piercing through the tip and the gold cuff that encompasses it tell everyone that I'm an alpha.

And yet, my heart yearns to be something else.

Alphas are dominant, omegas are submissive. Yin and yang, we complement one another to make the perfect whole.

Not all omegas are females just as not all males are alphas, but I've never heard of an alpha who wanted to be submissive.

It goes against what's ingrained in our DNA, yet here I sit, wanting nothing more than for Fern to push me on my knees, drag me around, tell me I'm her good boy.

My arousal intensifies at the vision my thoughts invoke, and I realize I'm sitting in a diner booth that's four times too small for me, with my tongue lolled out while panting loudly.

I have no idea how much time has passed. Fern is still standing at the door, her eyes wide, her cheeks flaming red.

Growling, I shove out of the tiny space, disrupting the booth and knocking the table askew as I walk over to her.

If everyone wasn't staring before, they are now.

"You look absolutely beautiful," I manage past the lust clouding my ability to function.

If possible, Fern's blush deepens and the scent of her arousal wraps around me. My inner alpha perks back up, demanding we take what she's offering.

Arousal doesn't equate to acceptance, I remind, and my alpha grumbles before going silent once more.

With a soft smile, I offer Fern my arm and escort her back to our booth. Her tiny hand trembles against my bicep, and the scent of her need is replaced with fear.

The stares of the diner's occupants unnerve her, and I realize that the people who are strangers to me are not to her.

The second Fern's bottom hits the booth seat, she scoots over, scrunching down by the window, pulling her red hair forward to shield her face.

"Is everything alright? We can leave if you're uncomfortable about being here with me."

Immediately, Fern straightens, a frown marring her full lips. "It's not you, Ahnou. I'm sorry if I gave you that impression. It's me. I just don't like being the center of everyone's attention."

Her kindness wraps around my heart. "Thank you for clarifying. I didn't think you were uneasy because you were with an Anubis, but I can assure that's why everyone is staring."

"Probably, that and I think my divorce is still a hot topic. Chet made quite a scene at the court afterward…the cops had to hold him back."

The alpha inside of me rears his head, going into full protection mode. "Did you get a restraining order against him?"

"No, mostly because the abuse was verbal and from previous years. When I asked, the police told me I didn't have enough evidence to have one granted."

My snarl rumbles out of me before I can tamp it back, and everyone within three meters startles in alarm.

Forcing a calm expression on my face, I raise a hand in apology. "Sorry! I saw the pie and got excited."

The diners relax, and a few even chuckle. One man slaps his leg. "Best pie in the state!"

"Smells like it. I'll have to try some."

Slowly, everything returns to normal, and Fern's shoulders loosen. "Please forgive me, kianga. Sometimes my instincts take over, but this is no excuse for me not controlling myself."

Fern chuckles. "I think after how I writhed in your lap this afternoon, I have no room to judge."

Her eyes widen as she claps a hand over her mouth. Fern's cheeks burst with color as she furtively glances around to see who heard her.

No one is paying us much attention anymore—*thank Osiris*—but my mind is now firmly fixated on the memory of the redheaded wonder gyrating in my lap until we both came.

"Ahnou?"

I clear my throat. "Yes?" She nods to the waitress who must have just appeared, waiting to take our drink order. "I'll have water, thank you."

The other woman nods, placing a couple of menus on the table before turning to walk away.

Across from me, all the vivid red drains from Fern's face, leaving her pale and shaking as she stares at the table.

"New menus?" she wonders, and the waitress spins back around.

"Yep. Ma and Pa sold the restaurant six months ago. The new owners kept the same name but revamped everything on the menu."

"Revamped?" Fern gasps, as if genuinely shocked. "Right. Um, what do you suggest then?"

The waitress shrugs. "Oh, it's all good. I couldn't pick just one thing!"

With this, she leaves Fern and me alone, the former looking like someone ripped the rug from under her feet.

Tears fill her eyes, and I wonder with everything that's happened in Fern's life if perhaps she hasn't been out much.

Maybe this was her favorite diner, and it changing is now the crap-cherry on the upheaval she's already experienced.

But the longer I assess Fern, the more I think it's something else. The way she squints, her gaze darting back and forth frantically as her lips attempt to silently read the words cue me in.

Fern struggles to read—and I feel her struggle in the depths of my soul.

Anubis are blessed with unique neural chemistry that gives each of us the remarkable abilities that humans often envy, but it also comes with a downside.

Because of our heightened perception, Anubis are more susceptible to sensory overload from our environment.

Since our brains process information at an accelerated rate, it leads to difficulties in decoding written language or understanding symbolic representations like letters.

On the one paw, this allows many of us, including myself, to detect subtle details that others might miss, which is why I'm so valuable to the IRS.

On the other, every Anubis experiences some form of dyslexia. As a community, we've embraced our differences and learned to help our cubs adapt, but it doesn't negate the struggle each of us experiences.

Even now, after years of training, I have to really focus to read with the fluidity that most people can do automatically.

Although Fern might not be dyslexic, I hate to see her distress. It brings me back to my youth when I tried so hard to make sense of the symbols, only for them to float around the page.

Clearing my throat, I catch Fern's attention. "You know, I'm torn between a few items on the menu. Will you help me pick one out, please?

The chicken parmesan sounds delicious, but so does the shepherd's pie or the cheese quiche. There's also shrimp alfredo or the breakfast cheeseburger, complete with egg and bacon.

There's a whole list of things you can add to it, like a sausage patty, and you can have fries or onion rings. All the other entrees come with a cup of the soup of the day and a salad."

I try to pick a variety, including something meatless, and hope one of them will appeal to Fern's palette.

"Oh man, I could eat chicken parmesan, shrimp alfredo, and cheeseburgers all day long!"

She loves meat, my alpha crows, and I suppress the urge to roll my eyes at his hormonal antics.

Finally, Fern makes her choice, and I signal the waiter to place our orders. With that settled, our conversation flows smoothly, and the earlier moment of Fern's tension dissipates.

We chat about our jobs, and I love the passion Fern has for her café. I could listen to her talk for hours.

The way her eyes light up every time I ask about an ingredient or specialty tea stirs the long-dormant urge to claim someone as my mate—specifically, *her*.

Anyone looking on wouldn't guess this isn't a real date. Truth be told, even *I* forgot, feeling more at ease with a person I met only hours ago than I do my own family.

Between our easy banter and the heated glances that linger just a little longer than they should, the romantic tension is palpable.

By the time we're done eating, everyone in the diner is back to whispering, and I have no doubt that by tomorrow morning, Fern and I will be the talk of the town.

Mission accomplished.

With a gentle touch, I reach for her hand across the table, our fingers intertwining effortlessly.

The spark of electricity at the contact sends a shiver down my spine, and Fern trembles, the scent of her need swelling over me like a sandstorm.

She licks her lips, drawing my eye, and I nearly groan at the sight of her plump, red mouth glistening from where she wet it.

"I know you wanted to try the pie here, but maybe…you want to come back to my house for dessert? I have a spice cake with cream cheese frosting infused with maple syrup."

Her sweet offer hangs between us, and I know if I go back to her house, the only thing I'll be eating is *her.*

An internal war erupts inside of me while I silently debate what to do, but my alpha wins—he always does when he wants to.

"Spice cake sounds delicious."

Fern's pupils dilate, and my khenen pulses. Breathing in through my nose, I will my hardened length to soften before getting up from the booth.

I lay down some cash—more than enough to cover dinner and tip—and Fern protests, but I shush her with a finger.

"You can buy me a meal some other time. Besides, you're providing the dessert."

The last part comes out in a growl, and Fern whimpers.

"Time to go," I hiss before I do something that'll really have this town talking.

Together, Fern and I exit the diner. We walk to her car, where I open the door and help her in.

"See you in a bit?"

"Nothing could stop me."

With this, she drives off, and I damn near rip the door off my tiny vehicle in my haste as I try to climb in.

I promised I wouldn't push Fern, and I won't…but I also promised her more orgasms.

And Anubis never go back on their word.

Chapter

Nine

FERN

Ahnou in a suit was devastating, but when I walk into the diner and see him dressed in dark jeans and a white t-shirt, I clutch the doorjamb, silently praying I don't turn into a puddle.

The bell over the door dings loudly, signifying my entrance, and all the heads in the diner turn my way.

Of course, I blush under the attention, but their gazes quickly drift away when I lock eyes with Ahnou, the monstrous man who probably will occupy the town gossip for a long while.

He gives me a cursory glance, but once his golden orbs lock with mine again, they're filled with heat.

The smoldering ashes of our previous encounter erupt back into flames, scorching my insides until I feel the need to fan myself.

After what feels like a small eternity of staring at one another, Ahnou gets up, jostling the table and the booth of the people seated behind him in his haste.

He tosses out an apology but never stops looking at me, and warmth blossoms in my chest.

As awkward and unsure as I feel, the only thing I can be certain of is that for some mysterious reason, this man wants me as much as I want him.

It's as if he's starving, and I'm the most delectable treat placed before him that he can't wait to gobble up—and how do I want him to swallow me whole.

The newly awakened part of me wants to spread myself out to be his personal buffet, but it's bad enough I've embroiled him in this fake relationship.

I probably shouldn't make things more awkward by asking him to feast on me.

An image of me covered in whipped cream with him licking it off between my legs fills my head and eyes.

As Ahnou stalks toward me, he growls. He says he can't, but I swear that man can read minds—not that he would need to when he can *smell* me.

Clearing my throat, I wrangle my inner dialogue and hormones until they are under control.

Before I know it, Ahnou towers over me, taking my hand in his and bringing it up for a gentlemanly kiss.

"You look stunning."

Thank you, Seraphina.

No one has ever called me that before, and it makes my toes curl in the brown suede boots that Sera paired with the dress.

"You don't look bad yourself."

My words come out stilted, and I want to smack myself. At thirty-one, I'm concerned that I haven't mastered the art of flirtation like everyone else around me.

It's probably why I'm divorced, and my only relationship was a dud.

Of course, Ahnou is too kind to point out how lame my compliment is in comparison to his.

Instead, he puts his paw on the small of my back and leads me to the booth. He straightens it and apologizes to the people behind us, who stare with wide, frightened eyes.

I want to smack them for being impolite. Yes, Cedar Peak Heights is a small town, and we don't see a lot of monsters, but that's really no excuse for being outrightly rude.

Sitting down, I give the couple who are friends with my mother a good glare. Immediately, I regret it since I know they'll tell her and I'll get an earful.

With a grimace at the thought, I scrunch down into the booth, hoping to turn invisible from the couple's judgmental glances—not to mention everyone else's in the diner.

A young waitress, still in high school, comes by to drop off some menus. I glance down, not overtly interested until I see the different shapes and colors and realize it's a *new* menu.

Dread surges through my veins, freezing me like ice, and it takes all my mental willpower to shatter it and continue as if nothing's wrong.

"New menus?" I ask politely, just as the waitress turns to walk away. She cocks her head, assessing me.

"Yep. Ma and Pa sold the restaurant six months ago. The new owners kept the same name but revamped everything on the menu."

"Revamped?" I croak. "Right. Um, what do you suggest then?"

My stroke of brilliance is struck down when she answers, "Oh, it's all good. I couldn't pick just one thing!"

The waitress walks away, leaving me to figure out what I want to eat. I stare at the letters, urging them to turn into words, but instead, they swim about as if they have a life of their own.

A headache the size of Texas starts forming behind my eyes, and tears prick beneath my lids.

I glance up at Ahnou to find him staring at me, his golden eyes boring into mine. There's so much compassion and understanding, I swear he knows exactly what's wrong.

But instead of calling me out or making fun of me, he pulls out his glasses and then taps a claw along the menu.

"I'm torn between a few items on the menu. Will you help me decide?"

Nodding, I swallow past the lump in my throat. He rattles off five choices, all of which sound delicious, and I could kiss the man for being so helpful.

Three of the things he read off I would eat every night of the week. I tell him this, and he nods, his gaze flaring with heat while I contemplate if I said anything particularly suggestive.

The sexual tension sparking between the two of us probably is an endangerment to the diner and everyone in it since it feels like it could spread into a wildfire at any moment.

Ahnou finally breaks the heavy silence. "Tell me more about your café."

"It's, um, profitable—I mean, enough so that I can put aside money for my taxes…"

That haven't been paid for two years.

My face freezes as panic takes over at the stupid thing I just said, but Ahnou waves a claw-tipped paw. "No, no, nothing about the financial aspect of your business."

He leans over the table until his snout nearly touches my nose to whisper, and my breath catches in my throat.

"Remember, this is a date."

A date, right.

Ahnou settles back into the booth, and I blink rapidly, trying to remember what the heck we were even talking about.

"Your café," the Anubis prompts with a smirk at my flustered expression.

"Erm, well, this is my favorite season there. I love making all the spiced drinks and pumpkin goodies."

"You remind me of autumn—vivid, warm, and bursting with color."

"My dad wanted to name me 'Autumn', but my mom said it was too 'on the nose' since I was born on the first day of fall."

"I didn't realize, forgive me. Felicitous parturition, Fern."

"Fuhlis-partuh-what?"

"It's how Anubis wish one another a joyous birthing day."

"Oh! Humans say, 'happy birthday'. Your way sounds so much more elegant, though," I add, lest I look and sound like a bigger idiot.

"I believe they also make cakes to eat to celebrate, correct?"

"Yep! This year, I made myself a triple-layer chocolate supreme cake with fudgy brownie baked between the layers, all covered in chocolate ganache. It was amazing."

"Sounds…*chocolatey.*"

"Very. Sometimes a girl just wants to lose herself in a vat of dark, velvety goodness."

Ahnou coughs, and I realize I pretty much described him and amend my first impression from tall, dark, and deadly to tall, dark, and *delicious.*

"Duly noted. I've always wanted to try chocolate, but it unsettles all Anubis stomachs."

"Same with dogs—" I break off, horrified. "Oh my gosh, Ahnou, I didn't mean to liken you to a dog!"

A soft smile curls the corners of his mouth. "It's ok, Fern. There are similarities, just like there are similarities between humans and apes. If I said an ape has five fingers like a human, would you take offense?"

"No, but I'm sure it gets old for you."

"It does, but I also understand these comments aren't said in malice. It just gives me the opportunity to educate someone about my kind.

As it were, Anubis share many characteristics with our domesticated canine brethren, and so it's only natural for humans to make those connections."

"Still, I apologize. I'm a lousy date."

Ahnou frowns, the sharp downward turn of his lips exposing the sharps of his teeth. "No, you're not. I enjoy your company more than I can say.

Usually, I don't get to interact with people when I'm on a job—apparently, audits intimidate and even scare some individuals."

I snort into my water. "Dude, you're like the boogeyman for adults."

He chuckles and lowers his head back close to my ear. "Watch out, or the big bad IRS auditor will come and get you."

It was meant to be a joke, or if I had a brain cell, a warning, but every nerve ending inside of me lit up at the idea of Ahnou coming to 'get me'.

With a groan, he moves away, shaking his head as his nostrils flare, and I blush because I know he's smelling me again.

Damn it, hormones, get it together!

"So, ah, what do you like to do besides terrifying citizens?"

Ahnou slouches down, running a claw along his snout while he grins at me, and I swallow my tongue.

Should a government official be this sexy?

"In my spare time, I like to read."

Instantly, a vision of him lying in bed—naked—holding a book and wearing his spectacles pops into my head.

"What types of books do you read?" I blurt in a rush to dispel the thought, not to mention the arousal sure to come with it.

"Mysteries, mostly."

I wrinkle my nose. "Mystery novels? Like Agatha Christie?"

"Personally, I prefer the classics. Sherlock Holmes is my favorite."

"This suits everything I mentally envision about you."

He laughs again. "So you've figured me out?"

"Not by half."

"Do you like to read?"

My face heats up so fast, I'm surprised my hair doesn't set fire. "Um, sorta. Kinda. Not really. Sometimes. So what else do you like to do?"

I take a big gulp of water while Ahnou stares at me, nonplussed. "I apologize if my question distressed you."

"No! It didn't…I just prefer watching shows."

My "date" nods. "Anything in particular?"

"Bridgerton."

"Ah, a fan of Regency romance. The clothing for that era is lovely, although I doubt I would suffer a cravat and breeches. Ties and a suit are punishment enough."

"Yeah, the dresses are to die for, but I'm fairly certain you couldn't squeeze me into a corset—and if you did, I would pass out à la Elizabeth Swan in *Pirates of the Caribbean*."

"We're going to work on that on our next date."

My mind blanks at the thought of us going out *again*. "Ugh, squeezing me into a corset?"

Hell's bells, I don't even care if I pass out if this man is the one to get the thing on me.

"No, making you realize that your body size isn't something shameful, but something to be celebrated. People come in all different shapes, and one is not better over another.

But for the record, I love every curve and dip that graces your beautiful frame. You're perfection in human form."

Someone clears their throat, and I startle to see our waitress standing there, her arms laden with more food than two people should be eating.

She plops it down in the center of the table, and Ahnou pushes the plates in my direction, urging me to start eating.

While his words absolutely warm my heart, no one else thinks like he does. Even my own mom calls me a cow, and I look like one with four different dishes of food in front of me.

"Ignore everyone around us, kianga. Food is meant to be enjoyed—so enjoy. Take whatever tickles your fancy."

Pulling the burger and onion rings closer forward, I reach for the ketchup. "This is the third time you've called me that, what does it mean?"

"Kianga?"

"Mhmm."

"It's just a term of endearment Anubis use, similar to the human equivalent of 'beloved',"

The burger damn near burns my tongue because I let it sit there too long, the hot juices dripping into my hanging mouth.

Everything that comes out of this man's mouth leaves me speechless. He acts like I'm something special when I'm not.

Finally, I bite down, a small moan escaping at the flavor of beef covered in melted cheese paired with the bacon and sunny-side-up egg.

Ahnou snarls softly, his gaze locked on my face as I eat. It's embarrassing how intensely he stares, but the obvious arousal warming his golden eyes ignites a fire of need in me.

Instead of looking away, I watch Ahnou dig into his meal, the pale pasta coated in a white sauce that smells delectable.

The way he uses his long claws to delicately pick up a forkful of food, the focused expression on his face as he savors each bite, it's all strangely mesmerizing.

Maybe I do understand the allure of watching me eat...

The rest of dinner passes in a blur of heated glances and me clenching my thighs to keep from lunging over the table to straddle Ahnou's lap and riding us both to completion.

A dangerous thought enters my head, something so bold and forward that I have no idea where it comes from—but instead of running from it, I embrace it.

"Um, I know you wanted to try the pie here, but maybe…you want to come back to my house for dessert? I have a spice cake with cream cheese frosting infused with maple syrup."

For a terrible moment, I think Ahnou is going to decline my offer but then a smile curls his lips. "Spice cake sounds delicious."

But the way he says it sounds like *I'm* delicious. An involuntary whimper echoes between us, and Ahnou growls.

"Time to go."

He flicks out a stack of bills on the table, not even bothering to count, before cupping my elbow and escorting me to my car. Liquid desire courses through my veins.

Screw going home, let's give Cedar Peak Heights something to really talk about.

Ahnou hangs his head, and I feel guilty. "So, ah, see you in a bit?"

"Nothing could stop me," he swears.

His words are laden with a promise, and it reminds me of his previous vow.

To make me come even harder.

Chapter

Ten

AHNOU

Electric tension fills me as I drive to Fern's house even though the luscious, little redhead isn't even with me.

My heart races as I follow her, my thoughts filled with the possibilities of the night ahead.

Arriving at her house, we both step out of our cars and all but crash into one another, dessert long forgotten.

I think we both knew it was just a ploy.

The banked hunger for one another makes us both ravenous, and I scoop the woman into my arms, marching up the steps of her porch.

Regrettably, I have to set her down so she can open the front door. She makes quick work of it, turning the key and then relocking the door.

Sealing us inside.

There's another pause as we stare into each other's eyes, and then Fern leaps into my arms. I catch her easily, lifting her until she wraps her legs around my waist.

"You make me feel so light," she sighs.

"As Maat's feather," I whisper between nips at her neck.

I remind myself that I'm not marking Fern any further, just giving her the pleasure she's never known and deserves.

Stumbling into her living room, I topple her back into her orange couch, her hair fanning behind her to blend in with the cushions.

With rough paws, I push up her dark blue dress, revealing the creamy expanse of her thighs.

They're thick, and her knees have an adorable dimple in the center of them that I lick as I spread her legs wide.

Fern pushes up on her elbows, her eyes large with curiosity and arousal. I nudge the tip of my nose against the center of her sex, and she falls back with a blissful sigh.

Already, slick coats the inside of her legs, and I bury my snout into her pussy, flicking out my tongue to lick it all up.

As I do, more leaks out, and I'm ready to explode at how marvelously wet this woman is for me and what I'm doing to her.

I work the pad of my thumb across her clit while two claws gently pull back her lips so that I can explore her sweetness with my tongue even deeper.

She squirms, tiny hands catching at my ears as she presses me closer. "Mmm, yes, right there—right there!"

In an instant, Fern comes, and slick gushes out of her pussy, drenching the couch and the lower half of my face.

Mortification dances across her features, and she tries to sit up, but I gently push her back.

"We're not done."

"But but but…I made a mess. Again."

"We can clean it later—we're only going to get filthier from here."

Her sweet berry red mouth pops open, and my khenen throbs painfully at the sight of her pink tongue.

"Lie back down."

She obeys me without hesitation, and my alpha preens. He thinks because she responds to us so beautifully that she's ours.

Keep dreaming, mate.

But it's hard to deny how perfect Fern is when she responds to every touch with a cry of bliss or shiver of desire.

The only thing my alpha and I agree on is that we want to give the lovely redhead pleasure—obscene amounts of it.

For the next hour, he directs me on how to make her come next. Our goal—to make every subsequent orgasm better than the last.

By the time Fern's on her sixth orgasm, I'm going to explode in my jeans. I'm not wearing boxers, and the denim fabric presses tightly against my khenen.

I need to come but don't want her to think that I'm turning this into something about me. Tonight is just about her, although I'm fairly certain she's too exhausted to come again.

Panting, I pull back, pressing a brief kiss to her knees once more before running a hand over my ears, which keep twitching.

Fern pushes up on her elbows, eyeing me with a furrowed brow. Underneath her, a large wet spot stains the couch cushion that I will definitely be paying to have dry cleaned for her.

We did create the mess, my alpha agrees.

"Um, wow. Sorry, I'm a bit out of breath. Give me a second, and I'll get up."

"No. Relax. I'll get you a towel."

"Wait! What…about you?"

I shake my head. "Tonight isn't about me."

A frown mars her pouty lips. "But…I want you to come, too. It will bother me if you don't. You deserve a taste of the same pleasure you gave me. I can do whatever you want."

Her offer hangs in the air, and I can't help but stare at her exposed lower body in hunger. My khenen pulses as my alpha howls in need.

"Can I come over your thighs, please?"

She licks her lips, her arousal spiking with every inhale I take. "Yes, please come all over me."

My alpha yelps in desperation, damn near begging to unleash ourselves all over her creamy perfection.

"Hold still. I want you just as you are."

"You don't want to do it?"

"No. You're the perfect canvas."

"For what?"

"To paint you with our cum."

Shit, my alpha took over, but Fern doesn't even seem to notice or care. "Oh, fuck, yes, coat me in it!"

It's all the urging I need to unzip my jeans and free my khenen. Fern gasps at the sight, trying to sit up for a closer look, but I push her back.

"You have a piercing! And a bracelet!"

"It's my khenen cuff. It covers my ridges."

"Ridges?"

I remove the thick golden cuff to reveal the long row of grooves etched into my khenen, a sign of my alpha status.

"Oh! Can I touch them, please?"

"Later," I agree roughly. "Lie back. I'm about to lose control."

Again, she immediately complies, and my alpha goes crazy. With fast, jerky movements, I stroke my khenen to the beautiful perfection of Fern's body.

She smiles at me, a naughty little smirk that nearly undoes me—and then the minx spreads her thighs, revealing the soft pink of her pussy.

With both hands, she plays with herself, slick running out of her in a river of need that I want nothing more than to damn up with my khenen.

Her eyes narrow and her grin grows when I begin to pant and twitch. "Does my good boy want to come all over me?"

Oh, fuck, she's appealing to my praise kink.

"Yes. I'm going to paint you white."

Fern tosses her head back, lost in the same erotic build-up as me. From the smell of it, she's close to coming again, and without thinking, I nudge her over the edge.

With my khenen.

I brush the pierced tip over her clit, and she spasms once, then twice, her mouth stretched wide in a scream of ecstasy.

"Of fuck, come with me, my best boy."

That's all I need to follow her with my own release. My knot flairs to life, and I cup it with one hand, squeezing it rhythmically as spurt after spurt of thick cum splashes all over Fern's thighs and pussy.

She really is like a work of art, covered in my seed, and I reach down, subconsciously rubbing it into her skin like a lotion.

Marking her yet again.

With a curse, I yank back my paw, but my alpha looks far too smug for my liking. Both he and Fern sport the same satisfied expressions, clearly happy to have gotten what they wanted.

The redhead sighs. "Best dessert I've ever had."

I can't help but chuckle. "Ditto, and that's saying something considering how I bet your actual dessert is amazing."

"Maybe next date you can try some."

"Tomorrow night?"

Her eyes grow hooded once more. "Tomorrow night sounds perfect."

Nodding gruffly, I tuck myself back into my jeans and race off to find a towel to help wash up the mess we made, but when I come back, Fern's already straightened her dress.

She's licking her fingers, and from the smell of it, she's cleaning them free of my cum. My khenen jerks, already hard again, and it only gets worse when she reaches to give me a kiss.

I could drown in Fern's touch, but too soon, she pulls back. "Can I see those ridges now?"

Her small hands flutter to the front of my jeans, but I stop her before she can unzip them. "You have no idea how badly I want that, but for now, I think I need to put some distance between us.

Not because I don't want to be with you, but because I want to be with you *too* much—and you don't want me to mark you anymore."

I don't add that I've already crossed yet another line, branding her with my cum.

Fern bites her lower lip. "Ok, I understand. But we're good to meet tomorrow night?"

"Absolutely."

"Can…can we get dessert?"

Fuck, the woman is trying to break me, but I can't deny her.

"Dessert is now my favorite meal."

She laughs, the gorgeous sound wrapping around my khenen and heart. "Until tomorrow, then?"

"Until tomorrow."

We kiss once more before I pry myself away, walking back to my car. When I look back, Fern stands on the porch, giving me a small wave before going back inside.

My alpha urges me to give in and follow her, but I tamp back his obsession. Fern isn't ours, and she never will be.

But I'm not sure who I'm trying to convince—*him or me.*

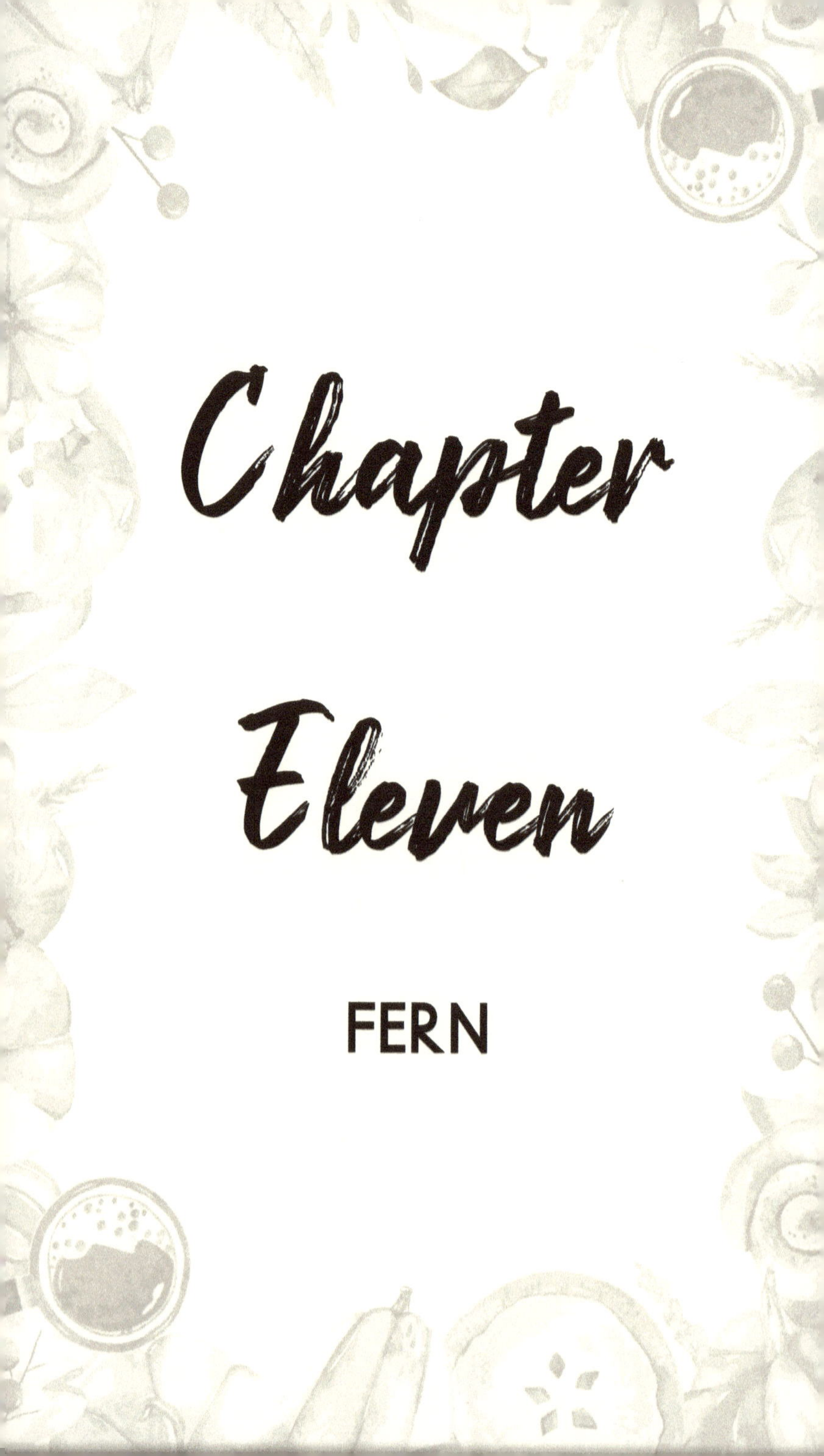

Chapter Eleven

FERN

Five days pass where Ahnou and I convince everyone we're an item while simultaneously pissing off my mother.

On the one hand, it's hilarious to see her so flustered. On the other, she's beginning to annoy me with all her pestering, and I've been avoiding her like The Plague.

The upside is that Ahnou and I keep growing closer and closer, but the downside is…we're growing closer, and I'm questioning if we've crossed a line.

How bad does coming all over a stranger's face who's supposed to be auditing you sound— probably not as bad as me telling myself everything is going to be ok.

That just sounds like denial.

Faking a relationship with an IRS auditor probably wasn't my best idea, yet here I am, holding onto the act like it's my lifeline.

I've attempted to create distance between the two of us, to convince myself it's all for show, but something about Ahnou keeps pulling me in.

Perhaps it's the way his piercing golden gaze seems to unravel my defenses or the unexpected tenderness beneath his stern demeanor.

Whatever it is, it's becoming increasingly challenging to dismiss that our 'relationship' is a mere pretense. Now, we're tangled in a web of make-believe that I'm beginning to think is real.

My thoughts spin as I work quickly and efficiently. I'm back at my café, surrounded by the familiar warmth and comforting aroma of baked goods while my brain percolates.

Just another thing that coffee and I have in common.

Seraphina bustles next to me, expertly frothing milk for a cappuccino while heating up some banana bread for a customer.

She shoots me a knowing look when I let out another sigh. "So how's the 'auditing' going?" She emphasizes the word 'auditing' with a sly grin.

"Honestly…it doesn't feel like we're pretending anymore."

My bestie serves the customer before whipping me up my favorite drink, understanding my need for caffeine in times of emotional upheaval.

"Sometimes fantasies can reveal the truth," she muses, her gaze focused on the intricate foam art she's creating before handing me it.

I blow on the steaming cup before taking a sip, the rich flavor momentarily distracting me from my tangled thoughts.

"Everything is so mucked up, I can't tell what's real and what's not."

"Love doesn't always follow a neat and predictable path, Fern. Sometimes it takes you by surprise, and you have to decide whether to follow your heart or play it safe."

My chest constricts—*love?!*

Before I can assure her that's *not* the case, the bell above the café door jingles as a group of regulars enters, greeting us with smiles and friendly banter.

It's another hour before we're slow enough that Sera and I can talk some more, but she studiously avoids me with a superior grin.

Brat.

The doorbell chimes again, and a man walks over, holding a thick, yellow envelope and a friendly grin.

I give him a polite smile in return. "Hello, how can I help you?"

"Good morning, ma'am. Is Fern Mabon around?"

"That's me."

"Ah, Miss Mabon, I'm Jep Wallace, the rep from Grounded."

Shitcicles, I forgot I was supposed to talk to the local coffee company to try using some of their products.

Between Ahnou and my tax worries, my mind has been in a constant jumble—not to mention my mother's antics.

I've only just managed to convince her that the IRS auditor returned to his office to look into my files, not that she cares. I swear she's more preoccupied with my "boyfriend".

Oh, and trying to get me back together with my abusive ex.

"Of course. Nice to meet you in person, Jep."

We've only worked via phone since email is out of the question, and I've halted *all* of my mother's involvement in the café.

"I have that contract for you to sign, but please read over this letter first, as it outlines some minor changes and stipulations my employer suggested."

Dread blossoms within me as I take the envelope, my heart fluttering with unease. The familiar trepidation settles in as I open the contents and unfold the paper typed in small font.

It took me a small eternity to read the contract fully on my own when Jep first emailed it to me—a week, in fact—and I barely succeeded. The legal jargon was barely legible to my brain.

The letters swim on the page, twisting and dancing like mischievous sprites, and panic anchors into my chest sharper than a knife.

Seraphina, ever perceptive, senses my discomfort. She comes up behind me and casually peers over my shoulder at the document.

"What's this all about, Fern? Some new coffee supplier contract?"

"Yes, it's with Grounded. I'm trying to support local farmers more."

She takes a moment to scan the page, highlighting the important parts out loud, saving me from the awkward reality of a grown woman who can barely read.

The tension in my shoulders eases, and I force a smile back onto my face as I pretend to do the same before finding a pen and signing the contract.

As it turns out, the changes are actually in my favor, but at this point I probably would've signed it just to avoid the rep finding out my secret.

Jep and I chat a bit more, Seraphina chiming in from time to time, until he checks his watch.

"Sorry, ladies, I have to run, but we're excited to work with your café. Thank you for taking a chance with someone local. We have deliveries scheduled starting next week."

"Excellent. Please call me if you need anything from me."

"Do you text?"

"I don't."

He gives me a funny look before nodding and leaving, but I already know what he's thinking—what person in today's day and age doesn't text?

I've always tried to keep my reading difficulties hidden, fearing that others might see it as a weakness, but I'm fairly certain that my efforts just make me seem unhinged to others.

The weight of my secret is a burden I've carried with me since forever, fearing that everyone will think that I'm an idiot if they knew the truth.

"Fern?" Sera's voice brings me back to the present. "You ok?"

"Yeah."

It's a lie, and we both know it. At first, Seraphina just nods, not saying anything, but then a look of resolve settles over her exotic features.

"No, you're not. You're lying to me—and yourself. You're not fine. Whatever's wrong has been bothering you since the day we met. I'm not going to push, but please know I am here for you, no matter what. We all have painful secrets."

"You have a painful secret?"

Sera ducks her head. "Yeah."

Her voice is hoarse with the confession, and I reach out to pull her in for a hug. "Oh, Seraphina, I'm so sorry. I hate that for you."

I mean it from the bottom of my heart because goodness only knows that my secret is like an anchor weighing me down more each day.

"Exactly! And I hate it that you have something painful, too. So why don't we help one another out? You tell me, and I'll tell you." I hesitate, and Sera rushes to add, "I promise mine is a gazillion times worse."

Rolling my eyes, I laugh. "A gazillion isn't a number."

"Yeah it is. Comes after a bazillion. Doi."

We laugh together at her dumb antics, and some of the tension from earlier eases off my chest.

"You always know how to lift my spirit," I murmur.

"That's what best friends do. Now, I'll go first in a show of good faith. But you have to promise me two things."

"Ooooook."

"Firstly, it doesn't change us. We remain besties no matter what."

I scoff, the notion so ridiculous that her secret will drive me away. "Obviously."

Sera shrugs. "Just remember, you promised. And secondly, you can't tell anyone."

"Done and done. I would have the same stipulations for you."

"Right, like you could have anything to make me not want to be besties with you—"

"That's what I was saying!"

"Ok, we're friends until the end?"

"Forever and ever, amen."

She giggles. "It sounds like we're getting married. Alright, I'm getting sidetracked." Seraphina pauses, looking around the café, which only has one customer.

He's reading in a corner and likely can't even hear us over all the machines running behind the counter.

My bestie bites her lip, still uncertain, but then blurts out, "I'm a monster!"

I wait for her to continue, but she doesn't, and I realize this was the entirety of her secret. "Um, why are you a monster?"

Sera squints, her brow crinkling. "Because I was born that way."

Another full minute passes with her staring at me before it clicks—she doesn't mean she's a monster because of something she did but because she actually *is* one.

"What kind are you?"

"Light Nephilim, or Seraphim."

"Wow…your parents really named you Seraphina? I kinda wish my mom went with my dad's name of Autumn."

"Yeah, subtlety isn't their strong point. Autumn is a pretty name, but Fern suits you better. You're taking this better than I thought."

"Did you think I would react poorly?"

"No, it's just people around here don't seem to like monsters much—like your mom."

"My mom hates everyone. As for everyone else, I think it's mostly due to a lack of exposure. Cedar Peak Heights is mostly human.

That coupled with the fear of the unknown—which a lot of monsters invoke—can create mixed feelings.

Besides, I'm romantically entangled with an Anubis, and you know the things we've done together, so I would say that I *more* than like monsters."

"You're right. You didn't start "dating" Ahnou until recently, though, and I've just been afraid to say anything—not that I think you're anything like your mom."

"Sera, whoever and however you are, I celebrate. I will always support you, no matter what."

"And I know this. I don't know why I thought you would ever judge me because that's not who you are. The truth is, I don't want to be Seraphim and most days pretend that I'm not."

A dry laugh escapes before I can tamp it back. "Then we have that in common because most days I pretend that I'm not…dyslexic."

I say the last word in a rush, heat searing my cheeks as I tell the first person ever my terrible secret.

"Oh, Fern, have you been carrying this burden by yourself all this time?"

"I mean, my mom knows—"

Sera growls—actually growls, and I instinctively move back. She catches herself, an expression of self-loathing flitting across her face.

"That is why I hate being a monster."

"Stop it. You startled me. You've never *growled* before, so of course, I'm going to react. Also, I don't handle others' anger well."

"I know. I'm sorry. I'm not angry at you, and I didn't mean to startle you—the sound just erupted from me when you said your mom knew because I can only imagine how she's helped."

"She has!" I defend. "She reads everything for me. If it wasn't for my mom, I wouldn't be able to function like a normal person, I swear."

"Firstly, you *are* a normal person! Secondly, doing everything for you *isn't* helping you—it's making you dependent, as well as adding to your self-doubt that you can do things on your own. Don't buy into her crap, Fern."

She punctuates this with a slap on the counter, and the only customer in the café jolts up in his chair.

"What?!" he shouts, as if just remembering where he is.

"Oh, sorry, sir! Can I get you a refill?"

"It's no problem. Just rereading *The Fellowship Of The Ring*. Why doesn't someone just destroy that damned ring?"

"Erm, I think you need to keep reading."

The man harrumphs, but settles back in after Seraphina gets him more coffee. She places a lemon poppy seed scone on the side of his plate as a surprise before coming back to me.

"So what kind of monster is a Seraphim?"

"Humans liken us to angels, but I'm technically an elf." She pulls back her hair so that I can spy the pointy tips that I somehow managed to miss over the last two years.

No wonder Sera always wears her hair down.

"An elf not an angel, so no wings?"

"Technically, all Nephilim have wings. When we get them depends on what kind of elf we are."

"So when do Seraphim get their wings?"

"Light Nephilim are the bringers of life, whereas our counterpoints, Dark Nephilim, are the bringers of darkness. They're called Teraphim. They get their wings when they embrace death, and Seraphim get theirs when they embrace life."

"Ummmmm, are you not embracing life?"

"Not exactly. I have to do something to facilitate bringing someone or something to life."

"Like planting a garden?"

"I mean, technically. This action unleashes your wings. The bigger it is, the bigger your wings."

"I still don't understand how you don't have any…"

"You know how you avoid reading or anything to do with it? I avoid anything that will bring out my wings."

"You don't want them?"

"No. Just like you want to be normal, so do I."

My heart constricts, and I reach for Seraphina's hand. "But remember what you said? I *am* normal, according to you. So if that's true, then you have to be normal, too!"

My friend huffs. "I know, I know, but it's easier to give advice than take it."

"Whatever you decide, I'll always support you, Sera, but how much of a headache is it avoiding 'creating life'? I imagine it's taken a toll on you."

"Probably as much as avoiding reading has taken a toll on you."

We fall silent as the man reading finally notices the scone and crows in delight. "You girls are the best, thank you for treating an old man to a slice of happiness."

Sera and I wave him off, happy to have made him happy, and it dawns on me that's how the two of us operate, constantly putting others before ourselves.

And how, deep down, neither of us are content as we should be.

"You're right, Sera. Avoiding reading hasn't worked out for me, and relying on my mom has only made it worse. She treats my dyslexia like a curse, and in return, I feel stupid.

But with Ahnou auditing me, I've realized I can't rely on"—*or trust*—"her. I need to find someone else to help me."

"And I'm that person. Anything you need to read, send my way, but I also think we should look into courses you can take to better improve your reading skills. What did you do in school?"

"Nothing. I barely passed."

"Why didn't the school do anything?" she gasps.

"My mom told me to never tell anyone. She did most of my schoolwork, and I scraped by on tests, which she excused as I didn't test well. Like I said, I barely passed, and everyone, including my dad, thought I was dumb."

"Your dad didn't know?! Cripes, Fern, your mom is unbelievable. That's child abuse, I don't care what anyone says.

When you don't help your child succeed to the best of their ability, then you're not doing your job as the parent. Shame on her, Fern! Look at how this has affected you!"

I open my mouth and then shut it, pondering what Sera said. "So why are you hiding your monster?"

"My parents were killed by humans who hate them. I was raised by my grandma but when she died, the only family I had left was a couple of friends of my grandma.

I call them my aunties. They live here in Cedar Peak Heights, well, one of them does. The other just recently passed, Denine Hubble."

"Oh, Denine lived down the road from me! Her sister Francine is a hoot."

"Yeah, Aunt Frannie is something else. I feel bad, she offered for me to live in Aunt Denine's old house, but I see ghosts and my aunt is still there."

"Yikes. Yeah, I would've passed on that offer, too. I'm sorry about your parents, Sera. I can't imagine how that affected you."

"Looks like we're both a little broken," she jokes, but tears glitter in her crystalline eyes.

"Maybe we can be one another's glue to help seal the cracks."

Seraphina swipes at her cheeks. "Deal. You heal me, and I'll heal you?"

"Are you going to keep prescribing me orgasms?"

"Hell yeah! Nothing sets the world right like an earth-shattering O."

I laugh. "Do you follow your own advice?"

"Nope, but don't let that stop you from enjoying your own pleasure—or Ahnou's!"

A groan escapes me because I had forgotten about that whole clusterduck of a situation. "Har-har. But thank you for coaxing the truth out of me. I feel…lighter."

"Me, too. We'll figure this out—together."

We hug, and for a moment, everything is perfect. Then my mom saunters into the café with a grimace on her face.

And my brief bubble of contentment bursts.

Chapter Twelve

AHNOU

It's been nearly a week since I arrived in Cedar Peak Heights, and it's by far my most interesting audit to date.

Usually I don't mark my clients and make them come until they pass out.

My inner alpha preens like a peacock, and I roll my eyes. The bastard acts like everything is set in stone, but when we leave this town, it won't be with Fern.

The familiar internal war starts up in my head, and I shut it down faster than a sandstorm sweeping through the desert because I simply can't deal with it today.

I have an audit to finish.

Not that this matters because I'm in Fern's living room, surrounded by boxes of receipts and records from her café, barely able to focus.

My mind keeps taking me down memory lane, reminding me of what happened in this room, and Osiris help me, I'm harder than diamonds.

This is the first time I've ever been uncomfortable doing an audit, and it has nothing to do with me being a monster in a human's house, and everything with the woman who owns it.

The alpha inside of me huffs in exasperation, like *I'm* the vexing one between the two of us, and it's not lost on me how we both pity one another.

What he doesn't seem to remember—or get—is that my relationship with Fern is a farce, but with each passing day, it's becoming reality to my alpha.

And that's why I can't let it become one to me.

Sighing, I sift through the mountains of paperwork, in awe of everything that Fern's done in the last five years.

She's built a successful business from the ground up and overcome obstacles that would deter most people.

In fact, statistically speaking, most small businesses go under their first year, leaving the owners in debt, but not Fern.

Her café clearly shines in Cedar Peak Heights if the numbers are any indication. Then again, I've tried her tea, and that alone speaks for itself.

It's not as good as her dessert, my alpha crows. *And by dessert, I mean her—*

Quickly, I jump up and try to remember the ceremonial dance of the Anubis on the harvest of Min.

It drowns out my alpha, but also disrupts everything I've put into order. With a huff, I go back to organizing the records into piles that only make sense to me.

As I go, I make notes of potential deductions. It's a meticulous process, but I'm committed to helping Fern come out the better side of the IRS.

Something that rarely happens when you're in the auditing stage.

Outside, the autumn sun casts a warm glow around me as the day wears on. The longer I sit and sift, the quieter—and more taciturn—my alpha becomes.

Things aren't adding up, he finally murmurs.

For once, I don't bark at him to shut up because he's right. Something's amiss in Fern's finances.

There are subtle irregularities in the numbers that raise questions. It could be a simple mistake, but my instincts, and alpha, tell me to dig deeper.

Even though I'm not officially Fern's mate, in my heart, she is, and every protective instinct inside urges me to investigate further.

I meticulously reexamine her bank statements, my gaze scanning each line for red flags when I note a series of withdrawals and transfers not linked to anything Fern's given me.

Knowing that her mother helps—a term I'm using loosely—I wonder if she has anything to do with this, but it's unfair to jump to conclusions.

Instead, I reach for my phone to call Fern when I hear the sound of a key turning in the front door lock.

Thinking it's Fern, I pocket my phone and step into the hall leading to the foyer, but as the door swings open, it reveals not the lovely redhead but someone far worse.

Her ex-husband.

We stare at one another, both of us clearly shocked to see the other.

"What the fuck are you doing here?" he demands.

The truth almost slips out, but I catch myself in time. "Making myself at home," I reply, knowing it's stupid to goad the man on.

"The fuck you are!" he roars, spittle flying out past his lips. "If you really think you can just waltz into my wife's life and take my place, you've got another thing coming, *dog*."

I stifle a groan at the unimaginative slur. "Firstly, she's *not* your wife. Secondly, it's *jackals*. Anubis look like jackals—although we aren't."

"Huh?"

"You called me a dog, but it's actually jackals that we're most similar to in appearance. Although, jackals and dogs are all part of the canid family, along with foxes and wolves."

"Are you too stupid to know I'm insulting you?"

"Oh, no, I understood, but since your insult was incorrect, I figured I would help *you* sound more intelligent. It's ironic, really."

"Call me that again and see what happens, you stupid, fucking mutt."

My brows snap together. "I think the only person calling anyone names here is you."

"You called me 'ironic'. Is that how you monsters say 'moronic'?"

Props to someone as smart as Fern for staying with this guy for more than five minutes.

"Listen, I don't know how or why you have a key to Fern's house, but you need to leave. She's not home, and you're not welcome here."

"This is my house! You're the one trasspessing—"

"Trespassing, I think you mean…"

"Don't tell me what I know! I'm callin' the cops!"

"Fine, call them, but you're waiting outside."

"You going to make me?"

Is this a rhetorical question?

Anubis are known for our patience and easy-going nature, but this jerk's hostility has pushed me past my limits.

Fully acknowledging the stupidity of my actions, I pick Fern's ex up by the scruff of his collar and toss him on his ass in her front yard.

Then I slam the front door and throw the dead bolt with the chain for good measure while keeping an eye on the unhinged man.

My alpha wants to teach him a lesson, but we're in enough hot water as it is. I have no idea how I'm going to explain this to Fern…

As if on cue, my phone rings. Of course, it's my redhead—I mean, not *my* redhead, but the one whose life I just made a thousand times more complicated.

"Hey, sorry I missed your call. My mother stopped by the café unexpectedly."

"Today must be 'Unexpected Visitor Day' because I just kicked your ex out of your house...literally."

The line goes silent, and my pulse picks up in speed.

"Chet was at my house?"

"Still is. In the front yard—where I tossed him."

"Did you let him in?"

"Absolutely not. He had a key."

"Agh, I knew it! My mom must have given it to him. Dammit, I forgot to change the locks!"

Again.

"You're not mad at me?"

"Oh, I'm furious, but not at you. Why would I be angry at you, Ahnou?"

"Because I lost my cool and got physical with someone...I've never done that before, and I'm not proud of my actions."

"You're one of the calmest, kindest people I've ever met. I have no doubt if you chucked Chet out of my house, he deserved it. I'm not worried about him, but what he'll do to retaliate."

"He said he was going to call the cops on me for trespassing. He still thinks you're married, and I'm the intruding boyfriend, not auditor."

"Wow. He's something else."

"Yeah, this guy really proves denial isn't just a river in Egypt."

"Was that an Anubis joke?"

"Kinda. I think humans use it, too. It's really lame, but I couldn't help myself."

"Honestly, it makes me want you even more. Tell me when Chet's gone. I'm locking up early and coming home to give you more dessert."

My khenen twitches. "Stop, you're riling up my alpha."

"Your alpha?"

I rub a paw down my face while keeping an eye on Fern's ex, who's kicking the trunk of the giant oak tree and losing.

"Anubis have a hierarchy we're born into."

"Like royalty?"

"Not really. I don't want to say how we're born has no effect on us socially, but it has more to do with how we are sexually compatible among other Anubis.

There are alphas, betas, and omegas. Alphas are dominant and protective. Male and female Anubis who are born alphas have different genitalia compared to betas and omegas.

Within us, we have a voice that we attribute to this. I don't literally have another person in my head, but sometimes, it feels that way since my alpha and I want different things."

"How so?"

"Well, remember how I said alphas are dominant, especially sexually? I'm…not. I'm more like an omega, I suppose, wanting to be submissive."

"Why can't you be both?"

Her question flummoxes me. "Erm, because you're one or the other?"

"Yeah, but in the BDSM community, some individuals are 'switches', meaning they enjoy being both dominant and submissive."

"Why do you know this?"

"Oh, ah, because after I separated from Chet, I thought to do a little research about the things I like…such as dominant men, but I also realized I think I like being dominant, too.

And when I say a dominant man, I mean a real one. Not one that's just bossy like Chet, but who knows my body better than the back of his own hand and wants what's best for me."

That's what we want, my alpha crows.

This is an A-B conversation you can C your way out of, I snap.

Unlike Fern, he's not impressed by my lame joke and just growls in answer before whispering how perfect Fern is for us since she and I are both the same.

"Ahnou?"

"Sorry. I was lost in my thoughts."

"Can an Anubis not be a switch because of your hierarchy?"

"It's not illegal or anything, it just goes against what's ingrained in us genetically. What my heart wants isn't what my body and mind want."

"Then why not give it both? If it's not illegal, I mean, or does your alpha refuse to let you be submissive?"

"He definitely wants to be in charge, but he seems to like the idea of you being dominant."

"Maybe…we should try that."

A growl of pure need escapes past my clenched teeth. "Don't say things like that to me. With my luck, your ex will call the cops, and when they show up, I'm going to embarrass myself."

"Why? Are you going to come in your pants again? Because that really turned me on."

"I meant because you're making my khenen hard. Why does a grown man coming in his pants make you wet, kianga?"

Fern hums. "I dunno…I guess it's flattering that you find me so attractive that you lose control."

"You have no idea how attractive I find you."

"Thank you. You make me feel beautiful."

"You *are* beautiful, kianga."

"My dominant side loves the thought of making you come in your pants, but my submissive side wants you to make me lick it up."

"Fuck, lock up the café and get home. I'll get rid of your ex."

Fern laughs, the carefree sound almost as gorgeous as she is. "Actually, Seraphina is here. I'll leave everything in her capable hands."

All the angst I felt earlier seems to magically disappear, even though Chet The Shithead is still outside. Then a car pulls up, and a woman steps out.

Fern's mother.

And suddenly, I remember why I called Fern in the first place.

Chapter Thirteen

FERN

All the happiness inside of me drains away the moment my mother steps up to the counter.

She's dressed like she's out for an afternoon in Martha's Vineyard, and per usual, I feel like a bridge troll in comparison in my black leggings and pumpkin-printed shirt.

Seraphina snorts but holds her tongue as I politely greet the woman who birthed me—and seems to resent it every day.

"Hi, mom. What brings you in?"

"Fern, why are you wearing such a hideous color? It makes you look like yesterday's vomit."

"How do you know what puke from the day before looks like?" Sera snaps, and I groan.

My mother gasps. "Rude! Why haven't you fired her yet?"

"She hasn't done anything to warrant being fired," I defend.

"Being impolite to customers is acceptable? Really, I don't know how you haven't been shut down."

"You haven't bought anything—ever—so you're not a customer," my friend interjects.

"I bet she pilfers your register when you're not looking."

Now Seraphina gasps. "I would never! Besides, everyone uses a card. We rarely have any cash."

Mom sniffs, clearly not buying it, but I'm fuming.

How dare she accuse my only friend when *she* stole from me?!

I open my mouth to say just this when I remember Sera doesn't know, and ever since I first called her, my mother hasn't brought up me being audited.

It's my hope that she forgets until Ahnou is finished and gone before I sit down and confront her about…well, everything.

Taking my tax money.

Giving it to Chet.

Having a spare key made.

Giving it to Chet.

Never helping me with my dyslexia.

Fuck, this list could on for days.

I cough, drawing back my mother's attention. "Would you like a pumpkin-apple turnover?"

"Gross, Fern. Do I look like I want to weigh as much as you?"

"THAT'S IT! LISTEN UP, YOU BI—"

Slapping a hand over Sera's mouth, I push her to the back of the café. She's vibrating under my touch, and I'm surprised she's not frothing at the mouth.

"In one word, how would you describe my mother?"

"World's biggest bitch," Sera promptly replies, and I laugh.

"That's three words, and pick an adjective that's not synonymous with bitchy."

"What's the point of this exercise and why are you making it so difficult?"

"Just answer the question."

"Fine. I don't know…dramatic."

"Exactly, the woman feeds off drama. One of the reasons I don't defend myself isn't because I lack a backbone completely but because I refuse to feed her drama llama fire."

Sera deflates. "You're right, but someone should say something to her! She's awful!"

"I know, but it's just easier to ignore and get her to leave instead."

My friend looks like she wants to argue more but eventually nods. "Ok, I'll be in the back if you need me."

"Thanks, Seraphina."

We hug briefly before I march back out to my mother. Luckily, the café is now empty since I prefer no one to witness the things she says to me.

"Mom, if you're not buying anything, then I'm going to have to ask you to leave. Customers are always welcome to linger, but only after they've made a purchase."

"We need to talk."

"About?"

"How you're embarrassing everyone by dating a monster!"

"Who's embarrassed, exactly? Because I'm not."

"Well, I am, not to mention how terrible poor Chet feels! Cuckolded in public, by an animal no less."

Rage bubbles to the surface that I tamp back with a supreme effort. "Firstly, Ahnou is no more an animal than we are. Humans are mammals just as Anubis are.

Secondly, I'm not cuckolding Chet! We. Are. Divorced! And there's nothing on the face of this earth that will bring us back together."

"What about your taxes?"

"Ahn—I spoke with someone. The IRS is helping me file the last two years and can set me up on a payment plan. I don't need your money."

She looks alarmed. "Fern, that's a terrible idea! You shouldn't trust your finances with the government."

"I don't really have a choice, thanks to you."

"Who's going to help you…" She pauses to lower her voice. "Read?"

"The auditor said the IRS will do my taxes from the last two years and then send me the paperwork with all the information. Sera will help me read. She knows."

My mom's mouth drops open. "You told someone—how could you?!"

"Stop it!" I scream, losing control. "There's nothing wrong with me. Stop treating my disability like it's the end of the world. You've spent my entire life making me feel ashamed."

"I was just trying to make it so no one treated you differently. If no one knows, no one can make fun of you!"

"You make fun of me. You tell me I'm fat!"

Mom harrumphs. "You are. That's not making fun of you—that's just being honest."

Before I can respond, a sharp voice intervenes. "Fern isn't fat! Stop body shaming her!"

Seraphina steps back in view, bristling with indignation. Everyone falls silent while my mother and best friend glare at one another, but Sera isn't ready to explode like she was before.

"Her body is perfect the way it is, and there's nothing shameful about having dyslexia. The only disappointment is the fact *you* never got her the help she deserved.

And still, Fern's never let that stop her. She's worked tirelessly to build this café, which is the most successful in the county!

Fern is kind, even in the face of your cruelty. You don't deserve someone as sweet as her putting up with your shit, and your judgment has no place here."

Red creeps into my mother's face, but before she can say anything in rebuttal, my phone rings. It's Ahnou. Just as I go to answer it, the call drops.

I turn around, wondering if I've lost reception, which sometimes happens when I'm in the café. I'm about to call Ahnou back when I hear the front bell ding.

Glancing back, I spy my mom marching out of the café.

"Good riddance," Sera mutters. "Why did she even come in here?"

"I'm not sure. To badger me about dating a monster and my taxes."

"You told your mom about the audit?"

Crappuccino, I forgot I didn't tell Sera the whole truth.

"Ok, promise you won't freak out on me…"

Seraphina groans. "Fern! You look like you're going to be sick. Just tell me. I bet it's not that bad."

"My mom didn't file my taxes for the past two years. Oh, and the money she was supposed to set aside for taxes… she gave to Chet."

"She did WHAT?! Oh my gods, that's worse! Please tell me you're going to press charges!"

"I can't! I promised my dad I would take care of her—"

"Yeah, but draw the line, Fern!"

Tossing my hands up in frustration, I try to verbalize why I let my mom get away with everything she does, but it just sounds like I'm making excuses.

"But Ahnou is helping, right?"

"Yes. He's going to file my taxes and then assess my deductions to help me owe less. He says I might be able to get a payment plan, even. Which is better than the alternative."

"What's the alternative?"

"My mom offered to loan me the money…if I got back together with Chet."

The words hang in the air like a noxious gas, and Sera takes several deep breaths before attempting to talk.

"That heinous excuse of a person stole money from you and is using the predicament that she created to get you back together with your ex-hole? I can't even, right now.

You better have told her no! Just the thought of Chet and you in a relationship again makes my skin crawl."

I roll my eyes. "Of course, I told her no. I trust Ahnou to help me…but I think I might have to shut down the café."

"What? Why?"

"Because I realized how heavily I relied on my mom to run this place. I'm actually surprised she did so much, but it was probably in a bid to help hide my dyslexia. Without her, I just don't think I can keep my business successful."

"No way are you closing Sugar And Spice! Besides, I already told you, anything you need done, I will help out with—no questions.

But we're also going to find ways to improve your reading skills. I bet you're much better at it than you realize.

When you've spent your entire life being told you can't do something, you obviously doubt yourself. And I bet Ahnou will always help with your taxes."

"Oh, Ahnou! He called. Let me see what he wanted."

Ten minutes later, I'm a hot and bothered mess as I call for Seraphina to come back out from the kitchen, where she ducked into to give me some privacy.

"I've got to go. Chet's at my house, making a scene on my front lawn—Ahnou chucked him on his ass, apparently."

Sera's eyes grow wide. "That is something I would pay to see." She pauses and sniffs. "Does the thought of Ahnou beating up your ex turn you on?"

"Erm, not really. Why?"

"Oh, ah, because you smell…horny as fuck."

My face begins to boil as I slap the palms of my hands over it. "You can smell me, too?!"

"Just faintly. I never did before, only after you started hanging out with Ahnou. I take it your Anubis is able to scent your need?"

If possible, my cheeks become even hotter, and I pull the collar of my shirt up. "Yep."

"Girl, take a breath before you combust!" Seraphina laughs. "There's nothing wrong with sex or feeling horny. If the man turns you on this much, jump on that ride."

"He's not a carnival attraction!"

"Didn't you tell me his dick is pierced and has ridges decked out in gold bands? If that doesn't scream 'fair food', I don't know what does."

I laugh until my sides hurt.

"Cock is not food!"

"Hell yes, it is. That and cum are one of the main blocks of the food pyramid. I'm sure of it."

"You're crazy."

"You love me."

"So much."

"Ditto, babe. Now go! I'll lock up, but only if you kick Chet's ass some more and have twelve dozen orgasms for me."

"Pretty for sure one hundred and forty-four orgasms might kill me."

"Don't know if you don't try."

I giggle some more. "Only for you."

We hug once more, and tears fill my eyes. Ever since my dad died, I've felt so isolated. He was the only one who really supported and accepted me.

Having Sera in my life is almost like having him back in it, too. And now that I've met Ahnou, it's like Dad is sending me a message from the afterlife to find my happiness.

I just have to take it.

Chapter

Fourteen

AHNOU

To my delight, Mrs. Mabon grabs Fern's ex by his arm and scolds him all the way back to her car.

He whines and gestures to the house, and I can't help the smug grin that stretches my face when Fern's mother all but shoves him into the front seat before speeding off.

Not five minutes later, my favorite redhead appears. Fern parks and gets out as I open the front door.

"Where's your car?"

"I left it at Francine's sister's house that I'm renting and walked. It's such a nice day, and I love the fall leaves. It's probably why Chet just waltzed right in."

"Ugh! I still can't believe my mother gave him a key, but I'm not surprised."

"She was just here. She picked up your ex and left."

"Mom must be making her rounds today. She was also just at the café. I told Seraphina the truth about her not doing my taxes. She's pretty ticked at me."

"Your friend?"

"Oh, no, I meant my mom. I told Sera something my mom made me swear to never tell anyone."

"Did you feel better after telling your friend?"

"Yeah, I did. It was like a weight was lifted off my shoulders. And Sera shared her own secret—she's a Seraphim."

"Interesting. I've never met one before, only Teraphim. He's a good friend of mine. We both have dealings in…death.

Listen, I've boxed all your tax records. If you're ok with it, I would like to take everything back to Mrs. Hubble's house."

"That's fine. I'll help you."

Together, we pack up her trunk, neither of us mentioning the conversation that nearly made me explode in my pants.

She drives down the street and turns into the driveway just as Francine is walking over. "Hello, Fern! Don't you look adorable! Isn't she the cutest?"

"She's the most stunning woman I've ever seen," I admit, and Francine beams.

"So this is the lucky lady. Well, no one deserves love more than our Fern."

The woman in question pinkens, and I'm surprised her skin isn't stained red permanently for as often as she blushes.

"I'm just helping Ahnou with something. I didn't know he was staying here, but I'll whip up a batch of snickerdoodles with cream cheese frosting the first chance I get for you!"

"You're an angel. You two deserve one another. I'll let you be, but Mr. Napa, please tell Denine to cut the crap or else."

I chuckle. "And if she asks, 'or else what'?"

"Then tell her I'm calling a priest!"

It's a bluff, but I nod solemnly. "Of course. Enjoy your evening, Francine."

As she hobbles off, Fern leans in. "What is she talking about?"

"Oh, her sister's ghost haunts this house, but sometimes Denine goes next door and messes with Francine.

Nothing too bad. Denine just flickers the lights and changes the channels on Francine's TV."

Fern giggles. "Even in death, those two can't be separated."

"Apparently not. Let's get these boxes inside. I've scanned most of the documents, but I would like to get everything saved and uploaded online."

"Ok."

She opens her trunk, and we take the boxes inside where Denine floats in the foyer. Her translucent eyes widen when they land on Fern.

"Ooooh, is this the one you've been choking the chicken to?"

Both Fern and I immediately start coughing. The pretty redhead turns to me, her expression a mixture of amusement and chagrin.

"Have you been, um, *you know* to me?"

"Can you blame me?" I murmur, not outrightly admitting to jerking off to visions of Fern seated on my khenen. "You can see Denine?"

"Yes. I've always seen ghosts, but it's just another thing my mom told me to never tell anyone. She was worried everyone would think I'm crazy."

Denine snorts. "I've never met anyone more obsessed with what everyone else thinks than that woman."

"Can you please give Fern and I some privacy?"

I hate asking since it's Denine's house, but she delights in tormenting Francine, and I'm scarred by the knowledge that the woman has seen me do private things.

No need for her to see more.

"He-he, you two lovebirds enjoy yourselves."

With this, she pops back into The Veil, leaving Fern and me alone. I rub the back of my neck, not making eye contact with Fern as I apologize.

"Sorry you had to hear that. I hope it didn't embarrass you."

Fern bites her lip. "It didn't embarrass me. It...turned me on."

My alpha howls as I try to remain level-headed. "We should take your car back to your house first. I don't want your mother or your ex knowing that you're here at Denine's with me.

Not because I'm ashamed of everyone knowing that we're together, but because they already harass you enough, especially with them having keys.

If you're comfortable with it, I would love for you to stay the night. There's another bedroom, but I'm happy to give you whatever room you prefer."

She tips her head to the side, nodding. "That's a really good idea and very thoughtful. Thank you, Ahnou."

Reaching on her tiptoes, she brushes a kiss across my snout that makes my khenen stand at attention, as if she kissed me there, instead.

I clear my throat, breathing far too heavily for such a small kiss. "Here, give me your keys. I'll be back before you can even blink.

Anubis are naturally fast, and I love running, but I rarely get to use my speed—working for the IRS really doesn't give me many opportunities to do it."

"That's so cool. I can't run to save my life. How fast can you go?"

"Last time I checked, I can run a mile in under three minutes."

Fern's eyes bulge. "Holy stromboli, I can barely *walk* a mile in under *thirty* minutes." We both laugh. "Oh, I have an idea. I'll time you. If you make it back in under three minutes, I'll give you a prize."

"What?" my alpha demands, speaking without permission.

Greedy bastard.

"It's a surprise—but it'll be something naughty," she promises.

My inner alpha damn near has a stroke. In a flash, I'm out the door, running before I even realize it.

Although it kills me, I drive her car slowly, adhering to the speed limit of the neighborhood.

But the second I have it parked and locked up, I zoom back to Denine's house. It's the fastest I've ever gone, and I swear I break the speed of sound as I crash back into the living room.

There, sprawled on the floor, is Fern with her hands down her pants. Her head is tossed back as she fucks her pussy.

The squelching sounds coming from between her legs are somehow even more obscene since I can't actually see what she's doing.

A low, rumbling growl works its way up from my chest, barreling out of my mouth, and Fern's hazel eyes pop open.

Her mouth forms a perfect 'O' of shock that makes my khenen weep, and then she comes—hard.

My knees buckle, and I slam to the floor as her body convulses, the crotch of her pants becoming drenched as slick drips through the material and onto the floor.

Like a fucking animal, I crawl forward and lap it up, my alpha riding me even harder than Fern just orgasmed.

She mewls at the sight, and I bury my snout into her pussy, inhaling deeply as she pulls her hands out of her pants.

They wrap around my ears, pinning me against her as Fern bucks into my face. Her movements are uncensored and desperate.

Exactly how I want her.

Chapter Fifteen

FERN

When I promised Ahnou something naughty, I didn't really have a plan. Before him, I never tried to be sexy.

I felt frumpy and unattractive, but this man acts like I'm a supermodel. Considering how he looks like one, it both flatters and excites me.

For him, I want to go the extra mile and do something special. Chet never encouraged me to explore my sexuality, either with him or by myself, but Ahnou is the opposite.

He wants me to know pleasure, and so I'm more than happy to give it to him back. He told me about how he's alpha but has submissive tendencies.

The last time we were together, it was all about me, but now, I'm going to make it about him, doing the things he likes.

I get so worked up playing the scene in my head, that I forget to time him and end up on my back with my hands down my leggings—and that's how Ahnou finds me.

The man's back in a flash, far faster than I could've dreamed, and it's only his growl that alerts me of his presence.

When I manage to pry my eyes open and look, he's staring at me with a wild expression. A low, rumbling growl shakes the air between us, and the sound is my undoing.

Circling my clit one last time, I crash over the edge I didn't know I was teetering on. A silent scream gets trapped in my throat as waves of pleasure consume me.

Ahnou falls to the ground, crawling forward like an animal, roughly pushing my thighs open even wider before burying his face between my legs.

I can feel the wetness leaking through the thin layer of fabric, and already, I'm desperate for more, but I remind myself this is for Ahnou.

Rising up, I pull off my shirt and toss it aside. The spruce-colored bra underneath is lacy, revealing the large pink expanse of my nipples.

They jut forward, as if demanding the Anubis' attention, and I'm too aroused to be embarrassed.

I push Ahnou back so that I can stand and shimmy out of my pants. He looks like he wants to protest, but doesn't say anything when the matching lacy thong comes into view.

With a gentle touch, I push him back until he's sitting on the floor where he literally licked up my juices.

It was the hottest damn thing I've ever seen.

His golden gaze watches my every movement, and I ease into his lap, rubbing over the hard ridge of his cock.

"I want to give you pleasure."

He snorts. "You *always* give me pleasure."

"Yeah, but I mean, with me being dominant, and you being submissive. Then we can try switching." His cock jumps, clearly on board with the idea. "Is that ok with your alpha?"

Ahnou pauses, assessing my question before nodding. "Yes, my alpha happily relinquishes his authority—but only to you. You're special."

I blush, which is rather ridiculous since I'm sitting practically naked in his lap, but the man always manages to surprise me in the best way.

And he called me special.

Now I want to make him feel the same way. Recalling our conversation from earlier, I squirm a little in his lap just to tease him.

Even though I just came, I'm a mess of need, and I can barely focus against the pleasure threatening to overwhelm me, but I won't disappoint Ahnou.

Besides, this is a perfect excuse to explore his cock up close. With one last slow gyrate, I ease off of his lap and point to the tent he's pitching.

"Take it out."

"My khenen?"

"Yes, your khenen," I repeat, testing the word on my tongue and liking how it sounds.

He does as I request, slowly unzipping his pants to reveal no extra clothing underneath. Instantly, his cock springs forth, and I whimper at the sight.

Ahnou snarls, and I quickly snap back to attention. "No! No making sounds that turn me on. Got that?"

His ears flatten to the back of his head, but eventually, he nods. "What sounds can I make?"

"Um…none. Everything you do turns me on."

"O-ok."

"Good boy."

At this, he bites his lip so hard, I swear his canine teeth pierce the tender flesh, but true to his word, no noise slips out.

"Pull out your co—I mean khenen."

Again, he complies, the dark length tapering into a red tip pierced with a gold ball that I can't help but wonder what it would feel like inside of me—not to mention the ridges.

I run a finger down the latter, marveling at how deep the grooves go, and Ahnou shudders at the contact.

"Fern…" he rumbles in desperation, but I ignore him as I eye the gold band at the base of his cock.

It's different than before.

Touching the warm metal, I marvel at what appears to be a much more constricting adornment.

"Does this hurt?" I ask, tapping the band.

"Not like you think."

"Why do you have a different one?"

"This is typically the band a male omega would wear. It's meant to delay their pleasure until their alpha releases them from it.

I procured one long ago out of curiosity to see how it felt. My alpha didn't like it, but lately, neither of us can function without thinking of you and being hard, so he let me try it.

Considering how it's staved off two embarrassing explosions of cum in my pants, I'd say it's working, although for how much longer, I don't know. The rut rides my alpha and me hard, and it worsens when I'm around you."

"May I play with it?"

Ahnou gulps. "You want me to take it off?"

"No, I meant can I explore it while it's on your khenen?"

Another gulp. "Sure."

With this, I lower my face into his lap, running my cheek against the satin smoothness of his cock.

It's gorgeous, the red tip shiny with arousal as fat droplets of precum bead out and drip down the grooved sides.

The gold ball that pierces the head is covered in the stuff, and I flick out my tongue to lick it clean.

Ahnou starts to groan but catches himself, his hips flexing off the ground to push his cock back between my lips.

I part them, letting him in a bit before pushing him away. "Sit still and don't make a sound."

A whine chokes off as he nods, his claws digging into the wood floor in an effort to not move.

Oops, we're going to have to fix that later.

"Good boy," I croon, rewarding him with the praise I know he craves—then I dive in.

With my hands and mouth, I worship every nook and cranny of his cock. First, I count the ridges with my tongue.

Twelve in total.

Then I lick around the gold ring at the base of his khenen before exploring down lower. Beneath the ring are two large lumps, too hard to be testicles.

"What are these?"

"That's my knot," Ahnou pants.

"Knot?"

"Yes, it swells when inside an omega to lock them in place as I come."

Swells?!

I can't imagine it getting any bigger, but the thought of Ahnou locked inside of me turns me on even more.

"Can we try that?"

"No, kianga. Only alphas can knot an omega. To do otherwise would injure the other person, and I would never do anything to hurt you."

My mouth curves down. "But I want you to fill me with your cum."

The words are out before I can take them back, and Ahnou inhales deeply in an attempt to not make any sound. To his credit, he succeeds.

"I can still fill you with my seed, we'll just have to be careful."

Nodding eagerly, I nearly crawl back in his lap before I remember I'm seducing him. "Later, for now, you're going to let me tease you."

Ahnou smirks. "Do your worst."

Scowling, I take the challenge to heart and pop the tip of his cock into my mouth. I roll the ball over my tongue, loving the feel of the metal.

Unfortunately, his cock is too thick for me to suck all the way down to his ridges, so I have to pull back and lick them individually.

As my tongue outlines each one, I'm surprised to find subtle differences in texture. Some of the ridges have raised bumps, while others have what feels like zigzagging lines.

Stroking along the grooves with my fingers, I press my nose to Ahnou's cock, getting up close and personal with every detail.

It's like a work of art, the way the black of his fur tapers off into dark, smoothed flesh and then fades into blood red at the tip. The gold adornments only add to its beauty.

"Take off the band."

"Kianga—"

"Take. Off. The. Band."

With a shuddering breath, Ahnou reaches down, his claws fumbling with the clasp that I can't see.

When it finally gives, the golden ring pops open and his cock swells even more, the tip now leaking a steady stream of pearly liquid.

"Such a sweet boy, are you going to make me feel good?"

Again, he remains silent, and I give him permission to speak. "Yes, I'm going to make you come so hard you make an even bigger puddle on the floor."

This time I can't stop the whimper that erupts, but I still maintain control. "Mmm, that's my boy. First, put your khenen away."

Ahnou tips his head to the side. "You mean back in my pants?"

"Yes."

With jerky movements, he tucks his cock back into his slacks and zips them up. Then I climb back into his lap.

"Grab my waist."

Instantly, his clawed hands clamp around my midsection, dipping into my generous love handles and gently squeezing my sides.

"Now bounce me up and down on your khenen and make me come."

I'm recreating the first time we met as the memory of that moment will live in infamy in my mind.

Ahnou understands the assignment and immediately lifts me up and then slams me back down.

He's panting, his golden stare pinned on me, and I adore the desperate expression written in their depths—a reflection of my own unraveling as he works my body faster.

There's no doubt we're both close, but I don't tell him to slow down. I know Ahnou can come multiple times, and he can clearly wring the same reaction from me.

Faster and faster he moves as I swivel my hips in time to the rhythm of his cock sliding across my core.

Even through the layers of fabric, it feels divine, and I yank him closer while angling my head to the side.

"Bite me."

"Fern, that's not a—"

"Bite. Me!"

He yips, as if in pain, and instantly clamps his mouth over my exposed throat, marking me like I wanted.

The sensation of his sharp teeth sends sparks of pleasure and pain coursing through my veins.

Barely even conscious of my actions anymore, I bend to the all-consuming need raging within me.

"Oh, fuck! I'm coming! Such a good boy—"

Ahnou snaps. With a savage thrust, he pins our bodies together as we both convulse, riding the high of the moment.

After a few minutes, he pulls back, creating a small measure of space between the two of us.

"You just had to make me come in pants again, huh?" I nod, a slow grin forming on my face. "Do you know what that means?"

It's a rhetorical question—we both know what it means.

Ahnou eases me off his lap, gesturing at the mess we made, although mine is much bigger. The entire front of his slacks are sopping wet, and my panties are physically dripping.

"My turn."

The Anubis punctuates this with a flick of his claws that unzips his pants. His cock springs free, already hard again, and I stare at the creamy white cum pooling around the base.

Before I can even lick my lips in anticipation, Ahnou grabs a handful of my short, red hair and yanks me down.

I tumble, face first, into the mess, and he growls. "Filthy little thing, aren't you? Making me come in my pants just so I can rub your face in it."

A mewl of agreement is the best answer I can give considering how I'm actively trying to lick up every salty drop of his seed.

He grunts after a moment, pulling me back up by my hair and flipping me around so that his chest presses into my spine.

Leaning us forward until I'm on all fours, I feel his cock nudge at the entrance of my pussy, and I arch my back in anticipation.

A large hand lands on either side of me while Ahnou pants. "Do I have your permission?"

"You can have whatever you want if you make me come again."

A strained bark of laughter echoes around us. "Not good enough. I want to hear you say the words."

Ahnou circles the pierced tip over my clit, and I nearly collapse. Luckily, he snakes an arm under my breasts to stabilize me.

"Like that?"

"Y-yes."

He does it again and again, the rounded metal ball bumping into me with the perfect amount of delicious friction until I'm about to erupt.

My Anubis stops, and just as I'm about to beg him, he slams into my sopping wet center with enough force to propel me forward.

His hold on me is the only thing that keeps my face from connecting with the wooden floor.

From this angle, I'm perfectly pinned under his weight. Ahnou repositions his left hand to rest by my head, caging me in, while the other stays on my waist.

And then he—finally—fucks me like I've dreamt about.

Long languid strokes where I feel every ridged groove sliding in and out of me until I can barely see straight, let alone think.

A litany of 'pleases' falls from my lips, and Ahnou snarls after every single one, sinking deeper into me, but never completely bottoming out.

"So close…" I pant.

"Come with me, kianga."

The piercing at the tip of his cock kisses the sensitive spot within me, and I unravel. My screams echo around us as I shatter around Ahnou.

Feral growls rip out of the man, and the ridged grooves along his cock flare outward, swelling to fit us even closer together, but at the last second, he pulls out.

Ahnou roars as he explodes, coming all over my back and ass, the sticky fluid dripping to mix with the mess I already made.

Neither of us move, breathing heavily. Ahnou finally leans forward to rest his head against the side of mine.

"I've never come so hard in my life. What are you doing to me, Fern?"

A bubble of laughter bursts past my lips. "Me? I think the question is the other way around—what are *you* doing to *me*?"

He doesn't answer me, just bundles me into arms to get cleaned up. Later, as we lay together and I fall asleep, I catch Ahnou staring at me.

His expression is so sad, a mirror of what I feel inside when I think of him leaving when this is all over, and I wonder…

What would it be like if he stayed?

Chapter Sixteen

AHNOU

I can't sleep.

Fern is curled into my body, deep in slumber. Her beautiful face the most relaxed I've ever seen, her lips parted as she breathes in and out.

Contentment settles in my bones at the sight because this is where she belongs. My inner alpha grunts in agreement, and I know I'm in trouble.

I've marked Fern with my teeth, with my seed, and now with my khenen. There is no going back. I'll forever be bonded to her, my mate.

But this can never be.

Every cell in my body calls out to be with her, but I will never push Fern into something she didn't consent to.

Even if I could go back and change things, I wouldn't. Having tonight with Fern to hold in my arms is worth knowing that I am going to lose her.

Another hour goes by, and I force myself away. The longer I lay there and inhale her scent, the stronger I reinforce the bond.

I already plan to do the unthinkable by separating myself from my mate—no point in making it more difficult on myself.

Thirty minutes later, I get the last of Fern's financial records scanned, and I make a phone call. My friend Ender answers, indicating he's earthside and not in The Veil.

"It's good to hear from you, my friend. It's been a while. How are you?"

"Eh, the answer is dual-edged. I'm calling with a favor, if you don't mind, please."

"Anything. You have but to ask."

As a Teraphim, Ender is not tolerated by many humans, who liken him to demons due to his enormous black wings, long beak, and sightless eyes that occasionally flash red.

But Ender is one of the most altruistic beings I've ever met. We've been friends since our time at the death camp as kids.

It was a place where young death monsters could go to learn more about their abilities, and the only time I was in The Veil.

I personally prefer to live Earth-side, while Ender prefers The Veil. It's where he was born and makes his home.

In fact, he owns and runs a camp that helps monsters who go between the two sides. It teaches them how to use the certain strengths that they're born with.

That the man is Earth-side tells me that he's on a mission. Ender helps monsters who are being persecuted by humans.

Either by finding the evidence needed to acquit them, or by taking them into The Veil to hide.

Being Dark Nephilim, he's one with the shadows. He is darkness, and nothing—not even human technology—can hide its secrets from him.

"Thank you. You have no idea how much I appreciate it. I need help looking into some records for an audit that I'm doing.

"Is the IRS being stingy in the tools that they offer to their agents?"

His question makes me snort. "When isn't the US government being stingy? But no, actually, in this case, I would prefer not to involve them."

"Meaning this audit is personal?"

"Why are you so damn astute?"

I can practically hear Ender shrug.

"It comes with the territory. So who is it?"

"My mate," I confess after a pause.

My friend whoops so loudly I have to pull my phone from my ear. "Congratulations!"

"Thank you."

"Why don't you sound as ecstatic as I think you should be feeling?"

"I'm happier than you can know, but...it's complicated."

Ender hums. "I'm pretty sure that's the definition of a 'mate'."

Chuckling, I spill the entire story to him. By the end, neither of us is laughing. In fact, Ender sounds just as sad as I feel.

"What are you going to do?"

"I'm going to make sure I set my mate up so that she's free of her mother, her ex, and from the IRS hounding her. Then, I'm resigning and moving to Egypt."

"Egypt? You could always move into The Veil with me."

"No, thanks. The Veil messes with your mind."

"Not if you don't have one."

I smirk. "That explains *so* much about you."

Ender snorts. "Minds are highly overrated. Send me over everything that you have so far, and I'll look it all over and see what I can find."

"Thank you. I meant what I said. I owe you one. Anything you want, no questions asked. I'll be there for you."

On the other side of the line, I hear Ender grunt. "That's a dangerous thing to promise me—what if I want you to do something bad?"

I roll my eyes. "Please. You're more likely to cut off one of your wings than to do something bad.

Just because you do things that humans consider wrong doesn't mean that they are. You're like a monster Robin Hood."

"Don't ever call me that again—and don't think I'm not going to hold you to your promise."

"Anubis never go back on their word."

I hang up with Ender, my heart heavy because I meant everything that I said—Anubis never go back on their word, and I promised I would never force Fern.

That's why she can't be mine.

I'm just recurling myself around Fern, indulging in the satiny softness of her abundant curves when Denine pops in, screaming.

"Fern's house is on fire!"

Instantly, my mate rouses, her short red hair in disarray. "Whaaa?"

Having never fallen asleep, I'm alert and ready. I grab Fern's clothes and help her get dressed before scooping her into my arms and dashing outside.

It's predawn, the sky barely lightening from its midnight hue, but it's not hard to see my mate's house, glowing brighter than the sun.

The entirety of it is engulfed with flames, and Fern cries out at the sight. I rush forward, holding her even closer as we approach the numerous fire trucks and squad cars.

Setting her down on her feet, I turn to a cop. "What happened? This is my girlfriend's house."

The lie rolls off my tongue with ease, but the police officer doesn't even blink. Instead, she reaches for Fern, pulling her from me and enveloping her in a hug.

"I'm so glad you're safe! We all thought you were inside!"

Both women burst into tears, and I rub my mate's back in an attempt to soothe her—a ridiculous notion while her house burns to the ground before our very eyes.

As if hearing my thoughts, the roof suddenly caves in with a thunderous boom, and Fern collapses to the ground, her horrified cries echoing around us.

Finally unable to take it, I yank Fern back into my arms and shove her head under my shirt so that her face is pressed against the warm fur of my chest.

I instruct her to take breaths, as my scent will calm her, while I glance at the cop. "I'm going to take her away from this. Let me give you my phone number to call."

She types it into her phone as I rattle it off and then nods. "Thank you. She shouldn't have to see this."

Before Fern can protest, I zip off back to Denine's house. She's waiting outside with her sister and a woman I've never seen before.

Francine waves me over. "Bring her inside."

I follow the women into Francine's living room, but don't release Fern from inside my shirt.

Her cries have turned to soft hiccups, and I press kisses atop the small patch of red peeking out from my collar.

"Fern?" the woman I don't know calls in a soft voice.

"Sera?"

Ah, so this is the Seraphim.

If I had been focusing, I would have recognized her energy immediately, so like Ender, but my mind was too preoccupied with my mate's blatant pain.

Fern's friend does the same thing as the police officer and erupts into great sobs. "I was so scared for you!"

"I'm ok. I was with Ahnou."

The Seraphim flings herself into my arms. "How can I ever thank you enough?"

"No need. I'd do anything for Fern."

My voice is gruff with emotion, and everyone but my mate sighs at my obvious devotion. Sera leads Fern to the couch to get her settled as Francine bustles off to make tea.

From the glassy look in her eyes, I know my mate is slipping into shock. Concerned, I step forward when my phone rings.

I don't know the number but don't hesitate to answer it. "Hello?"

"Hello, is this Fern's boyfriend?"

"Speaking."

"This is Deputy Jenson. We just got word that Fern's café is also on fire."

Across the room, Seraphina gasps, her extraordinary hearing easily picking up on my phone conversation.

Turning away, I walk to where Fern can't hear me. "These fires are no accident."

"No, they are not. We think she might be in danger."

Beside me, the Seraphim taps my shoulder, holding her hand out for my phone. I hand it over while she tells the deputy that she's safe, and I can't help but wonder if both women were targeted tonight.

And if Francine is in trouble.

I relay this back to the police officer, who clicks her tongue. "It's hard saying, but I would rather be safe than sorry. Is there somewhere safe and unknown that you could relocate to?"

On the other side of me, Denine waves a hand. "Oh, I have the perfect place! No one knows about it, not even my sister!"

A small smile tips my lips because I seriously doubt these two women have any secrets, but I tell Deputy Jenson what she said.

The woman doesn't even miss a beat that a ghost is helping, just makes me swear to get everyone to safety.

Denine whispers the directions in my ear and then winks out of existence. I march into the living room, scooping Fern into my arms while calling for Francine.

"Make the tea to go, we have to leave. Now."

Bless the sweet lady for not even blinking at my barked commands, and I want to apologize for being rude, but my alpha has taken over.

Our mate is in danger, and we won't stop until we know she's safe.

Chapter Seventeen

FERN

It's gone—all gone.

Watching my house burn to ash is like losing my father all over again. Every childhood memory, destroyed in a cloud of smoke.

My body is so numb, I barely register sitting in Sera's lap in Ahnou's cramped, little car. He's driving us somewhere, but I have no clue where.

The sun is up, and my stomach rumbles, reminding me that even in the worst of disasters, I can eat.

Moments later, Ahnou pulls off into a gas station. He has an electric car, so I know it's not for gas.

He goes inside and comes out moments later, his arms laden with various unhealthy snacks that I would never turn down.

"I knew you could read minds," I mumble in a toneless voice when he hands me a bag of potato chips.

Ahnou gives a sad laugh. "No, kianga, I just heard your tummy gurgling and thought some food might help stabilize the dip in your blood sugar that accompanies a great shock."

Francine leans forward from her even more squished position in the back seat—which is a generous description.

"Dearie, you're never going to find another man like this one. Don't let him go."

I nod because she's right—I will never find anyone as perfect as Ahnou.

"Where are we going?" Sera finally asks after she downs a granola bar.

"Apparently, to a secret place that Denine never even told Francine about."

"Hogwash. I know all of Denine's secrets."

Ahnou wisely remains silent. Instead, he gets back behind the wheel and starts driving in the same direction as before.

The topography changes a bit the longer we drive, the road becoming windier as the scenery turns hilly.

After an hour or so, Ahnou turns down an unmarked road. The bumps make me bounce in Sera's lap, my braless boobs nearly knocking me unconscious as they slap up into my face.

Just as I'm about to embrace the black void, my Anubis stops. I peer past the dash and spy a log cabin that has definitely seen better days.

Francine snorts just as Denine pops up through the center console. "You took us to Eckert's place?"

Denine's ghostly countenance becomes cloudy. "Are you kidding me? Eckert said I was the only woman he took here!"

"Oh, please! Eckert was a whore," Francine says succinctly, and Seraphina loses her cool.

While the two sisters bicker and Sera cackles like a loon, Ahnou tugs me to him—and through Denine—I shudder but am appeased when he apologizes to her and bundles me up.

I might have lost my house, but right at this moment, being in Ahnou's arms feels like being home.

Of course, my stupid mouth decides to say these words out loud, but Ahnou only stares down at me with his soulful, golden eyes.

"You're my home, too, Fern."

A fresh wave of tears flood my eyes and rush out to coat my cheeks. The sight distresses the man holding me, but I'm too emotional to explain how much his words mean to me.

Especially since everything between us is a lie.

"Come on inside!" Denine calls, clearly over her spat with Francine.

We follow her inside the dusty cabin that looks like it hasn't seen a human in over a decade, when in pops another ghost.

"Denine! My favorite—"

The man doesn't get to finish his words because Denine slaps him soundly across his face before hitching a thumb back at her sister.

I assume from the chagrined expression on his translucent face, this is the infamous Eckert—a.k.a. the old man whore.

"You have some explaining to do!" both sisters shout at the same time.

Eckert does the gentlemanly thing and disappears. Denine heaves a sigh.

"I'll go find him. Make yourself at home."

Francine mutters something under her breath before marching off to find the kitchen, leaving me alone with Ahnou and Sera.

Both look like they are silently communicating, and it's driving me nuts. "Whatever you two are not verbally talking about, just spit it out."

The two of them look like deer caught in the headlights, their panicked faces telling me whatever it is, it's bad.

But could it really be any worse than my house burning to the ground?

"Well?"

Sera purses her lips, clearly ready to do battle with me, but Ahnou grabs my hand and presses a kiss into the center before saying, "Your café was set on fire, too."

The darkness from before threatens to take me under, and I have to push it back with all my strength.

"Someone did this, didn't they?"

Ahnou and Sera nod.

"There are only two people who want to hurt me—my mother and Chet—but even this is stooping too low for them. What could they gain from killing me or Sera?"

"I'm pretty sure your mom would gain a lot if she offed me," my best friend interjects.

"Har-har, you know what I mean. Even I can admit the two of them aren't good people, but I don't think they're *murderers*."

"Maybe and maybe not. The cops are investigating the fires, and until then, we'll stay here.

"I'm going to check if the kitchen has any cleaning supplies. We'll get this place in shape in no time, and then I can get some food to cook for everyone."

With this, Ahnou gets up and sets me next to Sera. She leans in, her face serious.

"Promise me you'll marry him."

"What?"

"You heard me. That man is crazy for you. He's going to clean this place that likely has Eckert's cum stains everywhere."

I cringe, scooting off the couch to stand. "Thanks for that visual."

Seraphina laughs before she sucks in a breath. "I thought I lost you tonight. It was so close. If you hadn't been with Ahnou…"

"And if you had still been at the café…"

We shudder, thinking about what might have been, and I try to wrap my head around the fact that someone would want to hurt me or her this badly.

"I'm sorry about your house. I know how much it meant to you, as well as the café."

"It was my grandma's house, my dad's mom. It was where I first learned to bake. Grandma always made me feel special, and she praised me when I learned to bake without reading the recipe. She said I was a 'natural'."

"I know you have a lot of memories tied into it, but they're never going to go away just because the house doesn't exist physically anymore. They'll always be here, and here."

She points to my head and then my heart. Although Seraphina's right, I still ache at the loss of all my things—gifts from my grandma and dad over the years, the only things I had left of them.

Another wave of sorrow engulfs me, and I crumple to the ground, crying so hard that I can barely catch my breath.

In an instant, Ahnou is there, lifting me up and rocking me in his arms like I weigh nothing. He whispers to me in a language that sounds strangely familiar, and I ache to understand what he's saying.

Finally, when it becomes too much for my brain, I surrender and let unconsciousness sweep through me.

It's a sweet relief from the torturous pain I feel, and my mind becomes vivid with colors and shapes until they form into a person.

Ahnou.

He's smiling down at me, and he's stark naked. His gorgeous black fur glistens with what looks like oil, and I want to rub myself all over him.

Seconds later, I'm doing just that, and it feels glorious against my equally naked skin. I have no idea where we are or what happened to our clothes, but I never want this moment to end.

My Anubis strokes the tip of his cock over my pussy, the metal stud grazing over my clit with delicious friction that builds in my core.

"Such a gorgeous girl, all wet. Is this all for me?"

"Yes," I whimper.

"Mmm, I'm going to lick it up and make you see stars, but first, say you'll be my mate."

"W-what?"

"Be. My. Mate."

"Yes! I'll be your mate!"

"Fuck, I adore you. Now for your reward."

He dives down, his tongue replacing his cock, and I'm not disappointed in the least because he twirls it over my clit with expertise.

I writhe under his touch, ready to explode, but Ahnou teases me, working me to the brink and then pulling back.

Finally, he sits up, one claw circling the greedy little nub at the apex of my legs, soft at first, but then stronger and surer.

"Come for me, kianga," he calls over and over, his voice becoming distant but more commanding.

I'm yanked from my dream and back into reality, where Ahnou leans over me, his dark nose nearly pressed against mine.

My body is on fire, and when Ahnou whispers for me to 'come on, wake up', all I hear is the first word before I shatter into a prism of ecstasy.

Ahnou yanks me into his arms, where I grind myself into his lap, prolonging the bliss coursing through me.

Only when I come down from my high do I remember where I am and everything that's happened.

Instantly, my temperature plummets along with my libido as I apologize to Ahnou for making a mess in his lap.

Again.

Not to mention, I just ruined the only pair of pants I have.

"Hey," he whispers, tipping my chin up with a black claw. "What are you sorry for?"

I explain the dream and lack of control of my bodily functions, but Ahnou only tsks.

"I thought we went over that there's nothing shameful about how your body reacts. Just like when you're tired, you honor yourself by sleeping, when you're in need of sexual release, you give your body what it craves—and if I'm the outlet to make this happen, all the better."

"But now you're hard, and I feel terrible because everything came crashing back down on me, and I don't think I can get you off right now."

Ahnou snorts. "Firstly, I have paws. I can get myself off. That's not your job. Secondly, I don't expect you to get me off.

When you're ready to become intimate together again, we'll explore that then. For now, if it helps for me to get you off, I'm happy to make you come over and over again.

But I also want you to know that I'm here for you as more than just a sexual outlet. I'm happy to wrap you up under my shirt, cover you in my scent, and do anything to make you smile."

"You really are perfect, aren't you?"

"Nope. Just doing what anyone should for their significant other."

"You mean *fake* significant other, right?"

Ahnou winces. "Yeah, fake. Time to get up. I made you an early dinner, and Sera got you some new clothes."

He points to the foot of the bed where a gorgeous olive green dress complete with burgundy leggings and flats waits for me.

Leave it to Sera to turn me into a fashion queen despite the awfulness of our situation.

This reminds me that I was so distraught about my own crappy morning that I forgot Seraphina might have lost things, too, in the fire.

Since I have no idea how bad the café was, there's a chance her things are ok. Then again, all her precious family memories might have gone up in flames as well.

Ahnou gives me a moment of privacy to get dressed before rejoining me. He holds a wide-toothed comb that he brushes gently through my hair.

"There's also a toothbrush and some toothpaste in the bathroom for you."

Gah, this man is too thoughtful.

When I step into the hall, I'm amazed at the transformation of the cabin. It sparkles from top to bottom and smells like lemon—even the rafters gleam.

"Must be nice being able to reach the ceiling," I attempt to tease, but it comes off flat since I lack any true humor.

The sweet Anubis merely shoots me a little grin. "Sometimes. Other times, ceilings can be a pain, especially if they are low ones."

This coaxes a puff of laughter from me, and Ahnou's smile grows. He waves toward the bathroom, where I take care of my full bladder and dry mouth.

When I come back out, everyone, including Eckert, is waiting in the living room. The sadness on their faces tells me I'm not going to like what I hear.

But my heart is too battered to care—*what difference does a little more pain make?*

Chapter Eighteen

AHNOU

Deputy Jenson calls me while Fern is getting ready to confirm the fires were indeed no accident and caused by none other than my mate's surly ex.

I whisper this to Seraphina and Francine. The latter clicks her tongue, seemingly unsurprised.

"He always was a bad egg. If Fern's dad had been alive, I doubt she would've married him.

But Fern's mother really pushed the relationship, telling the poor girl that Chet was the best she was going to get."

Seraphina narrows her eyes. "Of course she did. I swear everything that comes out of that woman's mouth is poison." *My alpha howls in agreement.* "So do they have Chet in custody?"

"Yes. He's being charged with arson and attempted murder, but Fern's house and café were completely destroyed."

The Seraphim presses a hand to her heart. "The only thing I had left of my parents was in that café—and the only thing Fern had left of her dad and grandma was in *her* house."

"I'm so sorry. The only consolation I can offer is that Chet will surely be behind bars after this."

"Good, then he can't harass Fern anymore."

My sentiments exactly.

When the bathroom door opens and my mate steps out, we all fall silent. Even though Chet was the most likely suspect, it doesn't make it any easier to tell her.

Not to mention, all her worldly possessions are destroyed.

Things can be replaced, but the scars on Fern's heart caused by these fires will never go away—and that's what hurts the most.

Knowing that Fern is in pain, and there's nothing I can do to fix it.

"What's wrong now?" my mate demands when nobody says anything.

Serafina looks at me and I nod, silently relaying that I'll tell Fern. "Deputy Jenson called me a little bit ago.

It was Chet who started the fires both times. He's being charged with arson and attempted murder, even though you and Seraphina weren't inside during the fires.

With Chet in custody, it's safe to go back to Cedar Peak Heights, and eventually the police officers will need your statement."

Francine taps my shoulder. "You know, Ahnou, you and Fern should stay here tonight. Sera and I can arrange to have someone pick us up and take us back to Cedar Peak Heights.

We've been talking, and Sera agreed to stay with me for a while, and Fern can live with you in Denine's house—if she's okay with that."

Fern nods, her hazel gaze so sad that I wish I'd done more than just throw Chet on his ass.

Again, my Alpha agrees.

I look back at my mate, who's stunning in the outfit that Seraphina picked out. The olive green dress compliments her curves and coloring to perfection.

The only thing that I think she would look better in is nothing at all.

"Is that okay with you if we stay here for the night?" I ask her.

Once more, she nods, but this time with a little bit more animation in her expression.

"And don't worry," her friend interjects. "Ahnou bought all new sheets for you both to get freaky on!"

My mate's face blooms a fiery shade even brighter than her hair, while Seraphina and Francine cackle.

"What about Eckert and Denine?"

Francine waves off Fern's attempted deflection. "Oh, they ran off into the afterlife together—with my blessing, I might add."

"Oh, good. I'm glad you three worked it out."

"Me, too. I'm going to miss her, but eventually I'll be crossing over."

"Not too soon, I hope," Seraphina murmurs, and her aunt pats her hand.

"No, not too soon, dear."

From what I gather, Francine is all the Seraphim has left in her life. Unlike my mate, who really doesn't have anyone in terms of family since her mother is the worst.

At least I can be reassured that Seraphina will take care of Fern when I have to leave. My alpha growls at the thought, and I ignore him.

Standing up from the couch, I pull Fern in for a kiss, not wanting to get lost in my depressing thoughts.

"Let's go eat before the food gets cold."

We all go to the kitchen and tuck in while Francine regales us with tales of her adolescence.

It's a marvel the older woman has never been to jail, but her antics seem to amuse both Seraphina and my mate, and seeing their smiles is like seeing the sun peek out from behind the clouds.

When the meal is over, Fern and Francine clean up, and I hand Seraphina my car keys from my pocket.

"Here, you can use my car to drive you and Francine back to Cedar Peak Heights. It'll be easier to arrange for someone to pick up Fern and me tomorrow."

"Are you sure?"

"Of course. It's no inconvenience."

"I can also come back and pick you up," The Seraphim offers. "It's not like I have anything else to do."

Right, I forgot she worked at the café.

"Tonight I just want to help my mate forget, but tomorrow, when we return to Cedar Peak Heights, I'll help her make the appropriate phone calls to the insurance companies.

Because you lived above the café, there should be a monetary clause for you as well. One thing I'm realizing about Fern looking through her records is that she's very meticulous.

She does everything as she should, so I have no doubt that she had the proper coverage, if not more, for both her home and the café."

Seraphina's eyes widened in shock, as if the thought never occurred to her. Her mouth literally gapes open, and she points a trembling finger at me.

"I knew it," she whispers.

I cock my head, confused. "Knew what?"

"You called Fern 'your mate'. I knew you were in love with her—and she's in love with you!"

My pulse races at her words, and my inner alpha does a proverbial backflip.

"Has she told you this?"

"No, but it's obvious to anyone with eyes."

I grunt, my heart wanting to believe her, but logic refutes what she says.

"Listen, Seraphina, I didn't mean to mark Fern, and I would never do anything to hurt her. Anubis mate for life, and so I will never find another.

But I will never foist myself onto her, especially after her ex, so I beg of you, please don't say anything.

When her audit is done, I can leave knowing that Chet is safely behind bars, and Fern can finally be free."

The Seraphim sniffles. "This is why you guys are so perfect for one another—but if the both of you don't pull your heads out of your asses, you're going to miss the best opportunity of your lives!

The two of you are so worried about the other that you can't just acknowledge the simple truth."

"And that's what?"

"That you're in love! Good grief, do I need to get Megara to sing her song for you?"

"Who?"

"Uh, the leading lady from *Hercules*."

"Hercules?"

"Honey, I think you mean Hunkules!"

"What is going on right now?"

Seraphina shakes her head in disgust, disapproval stamped on her features. "I'm quoting the movie."

"What movie?"

She throws her hands up in the air. "Never mind! Just go get your mate."

I mull over Seraphina's words as she and Francine drive away. When the ladies are gone, Fern and I go back inside.

Pushing my paws into the pockets of my jeans, I rock back on my heels. "So…what would you like to do?"

"I kinda want you to stuff me back in your shirt like you did last night. Or was it this morning?

Time's gotten away from me, and I wasn't in a good frame of mind to really appreciate being pressed into your chest like I was."

I chuckle, pulling her close to me as she snuggles between my shirt and my torso. Her nose and fingers burrow into my fur, and she inhales deeply.

Copying her actions, I sniff at the bits of red hair that poke through the collar of my white shirt.

Who knows how long we stand there like this, content to be wrapped up in each other, when Fern finally speaks.

Her voice is muffled, and even with my keen hearing, I ask her to repeat to make sure I heard her correctly. For this, Fern has to move, but she doesn't get out of my shirt.

Instead, she just tips her head back. I look down the front, seeing just a sliver of her eyes and nose, and when she repeats herself, I know I didn't misunderstand.

"I want you to knot me."

My inner alpha keels over, and my mind blanks. The only part of my body that seems to function anymore is my khenen, which instantly gets hard.

It understands what my mate wants and is entirely on board.

"Kianga, even with how wet you get, you're still too small—"

"Can we at least try, pretty please?"

Knowing that neither my alpha nor I would ever do anything to hurt her, and that I'm completely in control, I agree—but only to appease her.

"Ok, but I highly doubt we'll succeed."

Fern positively beams. "Thank you, Ahnou! Let me go change into something else."

My heart skips a beat at her announcement. A few minutes later, she comes back out, dressed in nothing but an apron and a 'fuck me' smile.

My phone vibrates, but I ignore it. The world could cease to exist for all I care right now because the only thing that matters is being with Fern.

And thus, it would be hours before I see Ender's text.

Meet me in The Veil—it's an emergency.

Chapter

Nineteen

FERN

When I asked Ahnou to knot me, I knew he only agreed to appease me, but I'm not giving up so easily.

Sera, the minx, left a small bag of clothing for tomorrow that also contained lingerie and a pink apron with polka dots.

It's nearly identical to my old one, and sorrow clashes with gratitude at her thoughtfulness. Although it's not her intention, I slip it on after removing my clothes.

Lingerie can wait for another night.

The expression on Ahnou's face when I return tells me I made the right choice, his mouth popping open as his tongue lolls out.

I squirm at the sight, eager for all the things he does to me with the rough, pink appendage, and I grin at the thought as I saunter over.

"My jeans just became very uncomfortable," he murmurs as I stand on my tiptoes for a kiss.

He punctuates it with a lick across my lips, and I shiver. Between my legs, the familiar ache blooms that only Ahnou can fix.

With a paw, he cups my sex, and my head falls back as the pads of his fingers brush across my clit.

I tremble, slightly embarrassed that I'm already about to come. Every time I'm around this man, he elicits this reaction from me.

But it's more than just need—Ahnou lights up every part of my body, including my heart.

"Every time I see you, you're more and more breathtaking, kianga."

My chest constricts at his compliment, and I turn to mush. Tears sting my eyes because everything is so perfect about him—us—that I can barely stand that it's not real.

Because I want him to be mine for forever.

"What do you need?"

"Please make me feel good. You always do."

His attention is the perfect balm to my tattered and torn soul. Ahnou doesn't say anything but holds me closer and works his clawed fingers faster.

Sparks of pleasure ping through my body at the contact, but it's the look in his gaze that makes my knees buckle.

The golden orbs of his eyes damn near glow with the same fire that I swear is sweeping through my body. His lips quirk into a wicked smirk when I whimper.

"Something on your mind?"

I bite my lip before blurting, "Talk dirty to me."

Ahnou chuckles, the dark sound nearly sending me over the edge. "Does my kianga want me to whisper filthy things in her ear until she comes all over my hand?"

He leans forward and nips my ear. "I love when you're nothing but a mess of slick and need that's all for me.

Even now, you're drenched. Are you going to be my good girl and come so I can lick it all up?"

Oh, fuck, so close.

"Come for me, kianga. I want to watch those stars burst in your eyes when you do."

The command does me in, and I give him—and his alpha—exactly what we all crave. My orgasm explodes from the center out, slowly engulfing me from head to toe.

My sex continues to flutter, even with the aftershocks, and already I'm desperate for more.

"More."

Ahnou sucks in a breath. "Anything. I have an idea. Stay put."

He gently sets me on my feet and waits until I'm stable before dashing away. In seconds, he returns, his arms laden with various containers.

"Seraphina bought this for dessert tonight, but we never got around to it. She said you weren't a big fan of commercial toppings, but she also thought you wouldn't want to make anything, so she got a few along with some ice cream."

"Um…ok?" I'm confused, wondering if he's suggesting we pause to eat dessert.

My Anubis sets down a bottle of whipped cream, chocolate syrup, and caramel sauce on the coffee table.

"Oh, I forgot one. Be right back."

Again, he runs into the kitchen, returning with a reddish-pink bottle of what appears to be strawberry topping.

"Perfect, which should we try first?"

"Erm, the whipped cream?" I suggest, the idea of just eating it from the container growing on me.

I pop my mouth open, and Ahnou squirts some in my mouth while I moan against the sweet flavor coating my tongue.

When I go to ask for more, he's already there, but instead of putting it where I want, Ahnou squeezes the fluffy, cold treat along the neckline of my apron.

"Oops," he growls.

In a flash, he leans forward and licks me clean, and I moan. He does it again, and I finally catch onto the game.

Better late than never.

"Here, I think it might be better if I take off the apron so you don't accidentally get any on it."

"Good idea, kianga. I'm so clumsy tonight."

As if to punctuate his words, Ahnou dispenses the whipped cream down the line of my cleavage. With a soft snarl, he buries his snout between my breasts.

The whipped cream goes everywhere, and I instinctively grab onto his ears, pinning him to my chest where he laps at me until I'm clean.

"More?"

I nod mutely, unable to form words because the thoughts bombarding my head are too naughty to verbalize.

"What are you thinking about? Your expression just changed, and the scent of your arousal doubled."

"Um, nothing."

Another little chuckle that sends tingles down my arms. This man is far too sexy to just be on the loose around the general population.

How many women have turned into puddles because of him?

I scowl at this because I want to be the only puddle of need he creates, and that alone is a ridiculous thought.

Because none of this is real—it's all an act—but it sure as heck doesn't feel like one right now.

"Liar. Come on, tell me what you're thinking, kianga. I love every naughty thing that pops into your head."

"O-ok. When you put the whipped cream between my boobs, it made me think of you rubbing your khenen between them with it."

Ahnou whips off his t-shirt, and my girly parts weep at the sight of the perfection before me, his dark fur thinning to reveal the muscled definition of his stomach.

The only abs I'll ever have is the abs-olute lack of control I have around food—and apparently, this man.

Next, he slips off his jeans. Again, he's wearing no type of underwear, and my mouth waters as his cock juts out.

Tonight, he's wearing *two* golden bands as well as the gilded cuff that molds to his ridges. To make matters worse—*better?*—he's changed the piercing at the tip from a ball to a hoop like the one in his ear.

How does he expect me to walk away and function when he leaves?

The man's ruined other men and cocks for me.

"I've never seen anything so pretty."

Ahnou hums, the sound washing over me. "Likewise."

He grabs the can of whipped cream and a blanket that he spreads onto the floor before directing me to lie down.

Naked, I do as he instructs and squeal when he twirls the cold cream over my nipples with a flourish. Then he squirts another line between my breasts.

For a moment, he just stares. After a beat, Ahnou sinks to his knees, one on either side of my torso, his tall frame caging me in.

His khenen looms over me as he removes the gold cuff, leaving the bands and piercing. The cherry-kissed tip shines with precum, and I lick my lips, wanting a taste.

Ahnou hisses when he pushes the head of his cock between the press of my cleavage, the length scooping the whipped cream away.

He pulls back and then pushes forward again until he's steadily fucking my chest in sure strokes that make us both pant.

"What do you want, kianga?"

This time, I don't hesitate to tell him. "Come all over my breasts and make me lick it all up."

His pupils dilate, and Ahnou tips back his head. With a howl, he erupts with thick ropes of cum that rain down to cover me from neck to belly button.

With one hand, he scoops up the mess and feeds me the sweet and salty mixture until I lick each claw clean.

Ahnou shudders, his cock still hard and dripping. Cum coats the piercing at the tip, and I sit up to suck it off, catching the hoop between my teeth and pushing my tongue through the hole.

"More?"

"More," I demand.

My Anubis gets up and grabs the three other toppings. He pauses to spread my legs wide before ripping off the lids and showering me with sticky, sugary syrup.

The cold liquid splashes over my pussy and thighs, and I shiver at the contact as it slowly drips into places I'm not sure syrup should go…

Above me, Ahnou smirks. "Mmm, a Fern Sundae, my favorite dessert."

I laugh at his silliness but it quickly morphs into pleasure when he gets back on his knees and buries his face between my legs.

With the same hunger as I had, he licks me clean, even the sauce that leaked down into my ass.

I try to shimmy away, embarrassed, but Ahnou just holds me still, leaving no place unexplored by his tongue.

And when it's all gone, he feasts on my pussy like a starving man, and I explode in a tidal wave of pleasure as his clever tongue and fingers work me into another earth-shattering orgasm.

My whole body lights up in ecstasy, and I wish I could bottle the sensation up—hell, I wish I could bottle Ahnou up and keep him with me forever.

He gives me one last lick and then stretches to lay beside me. "How is it you get more addictive every time I taste you?"

I snort. "Don't think I don't know what you're trying to do!"

He cocks a brow. "What am I trying to do?"

"Distracting me with sweets and orgasms."

Ahnou laughs. "Distracting you from what, exactly?"

"You promised to knot me."

"No, I promised to *try*."

"But you have to really try."

"I will, but I won't hurt you."

"Why do you think I trust you so much?"

He yips, nipping at my neck. "My alpha loves that—so do I. You make us both so very happy. You have no idea how badly we want to knot you."

"Then do it," I demand, kissing along his snout.

Another damned sigh later, I lose my patience and roll on top of him. I spread my legs so that I'm straddling him while plastering my chest to his.

His khenen rests between the cheeks of my ass, and I wiggle against it, loving the feel of the gold bands at the base.

"Please."

Ahnou groans. "Don't beg, kianga."

It's a warning and invitation all rolled into one, and I grin, feeling mischievous.

With another jiggle of my ass, I pout down at him. "Please, pretty please."

His eyes narrow, the gilded liner nearly coming together, and I wonder what it is since I've never seen him without it.

Natural, a tattoo, really awesome eyeliner, does it matter right now?

"You're riling up my alpha."

Feeling bratty, I wrinkle my nose in faux disdain. "I doubt it considering how you're not even fucking me—"

In one smooth motion, he rolls me from top to bottom, his large frame descending on top of mine as he notches his cock at my dripping entrance.

"Don't bait my alpha—you might get more than you bargained for."

That's what I'm hoping.

As if reading my mind, Ahnou snarls and with a quick thrust, pushes deep inside my pussy.

The golden hoop feels different than the ball, and I savor the sensation as it and his ridges slide in and out.

He fucks me in earnest, but only goes three-fourths of the way in, just enough so I get every ridged groove of his cock, but not all the way to the base.

Ahnou catches my pout and kisses it off my lips before running a claw over my clit. In perfect time, he strokes it in tandem with his thrusts, and another orgasm builds in my core.

When I shatter, my Anubis doesn't stop fucking me. In fact, I swear he just pushes me into another release, and I come so hard, my butt slips from the amount of wetness leaking from my pussy.

He does this three more times, and my whole body is shaking from a combination of pleasure and exhaustion.

To my surprise, Ahnou pulls back, taking me with him, until I'm seated in his lap. From this angle, I sink even lower on his cock, the edge of the first golden band just touching my outer lips.

"Are you sure you want to try?"

I nod.

"You're not too tired? I had to make sure you're wet enough to even try."

"Not tired…but I'm pretty sure I'm wet enough."

Ahnou snarls. "The wetter, the better."

I giggle. "That should be a t-shirt saying."

He snorts. "I'm sure it is. Kianga, promise to tell me if I'm hurting you."

"I promise."

"Good girl." My pussy flutters at his praise. "Grab my shoulders and hold on."

Not needing to be told twice, I wrap a hand over each side just as he grips my thick waist and pulls me up—and then slams me back down.

The rough movement rips a scream from my lips. "Ah, don't stop, please fuck me harder—faster."

"Whatever my mate wants."

My jumbled brain notes Ahnou called me his 'mate' but I'm too far gone to analyze the slip up because with every thrust, he gets deeper and deeper.

When my pussy swallows the first gold band, I come. By the time the second enters me, I'm a quivering mess, and Ahnou is no better.

Sweat dots the short fur along his brow as he tries to hold back, but I want him just as wild and crazy as I feel.

I whisper this, kissing his snout before nipping at his throat like he does to me, almost as if I'm marking him, too.

He loses it, and to my surprise, holds nothing back as he jackhammers into my pussy with enough force to make my teeth clack together.

Another orgasm forms, and I know it's going to be a big one—the biggest yet. I whimper, locking my gaze onto my Anubis, silently pouring everything I feel for him into that look.

Ahnou growls, his khenen starting to vibrate within me, and I come.

Hard.

There's a heavy pressure pressing into my pussy and ass that seems to swell before a pop rends the air and I drop down completely onto his cock, knot and all.

Through my bliss, Ahnou's cock kicks deep inside of me as he follows me over the edge, spurting his seed as his ridges seem to flare out and rub inside of me.

His cock doesn't stop vibrating for nearly ten minutes, and I come two more times and lose consciousness.

When I open my eyes, Ahnou is still holding me in the same position, panting heavily, an expression of panic on his face.

"What's wrong?"

"Are you ok?"

"Yes, why wouldn't I be? I mean, I almost died of pleasure, but I'll take that risk any day of the week."

Ahnou huffs out a little laugh. "We need to sit like this for a moment until my knot releases."

His words dawn on me. "We did it?!"

He shakes his head in awe. "Somehow, you took my knot."

"That's the pressure I felt, wasn't it?"

"Did it hurt you?"

"No! It felt…perfect. You feel perfect inside of me."

Ahnou groans. "Stop. We both need rest, and I won't be able to keep my paws off of you if you say things like that."

I shrug. "It's the truth. I've never come so much in my entire life."

Glancing down between our connected bodies, I note my stomach bulges even more than normal, and I shift self-consciously.

But because Ahnou and I are still joined, I can't really move or adjust my body. Of course, my Anubis picks up on my distress.

"What's wrong, kianga?"

"Nothing, really, this just isn't the most flattering position for my body."

He scowls. "Every position is flattering for your body, and I want to fuck in them all."

I smile. "You always know what to say to make me feel better. I was just thinking how my tummy is sticking out even more this way, though."

"Ah, I understand now. That's because you're full of my cum. Fuck, we have to stop talking about it, or I'll end up knotting you again."

"Yes, please!"

Ahnou chuckles. "Not tonight. We both need rest. Kianga, are you on birth control?"

"Yes. I never wanted kids with Chet—not that I don't love children. I do. I just wasn't happy in my marriage and didn't want to bring a child into that unhappiness."

"I understand. I'm sorry he's brought you such sorrow, but he can't hurt you anymore. Come on, let's get cleaned up and ready for bed."

"Ok."

He still doesn't move, and a second later, the fullness in my pussy declines a little as his knot releases and he pulls free of me entirely.

Without him deep inside of me, I feel bereft, but Ahnou wraps me up in his arms, cuddling me to his chest, and the pain of our separation abates a bit.

In the shower, he washes me until neither of us are sticky and then dries me off before tucking me in bed.

I drift to sleep, content despite all the crappy reality of my life, because when I'm with Ahnou, nothing else seems to matter—when I'm with him, I'm home.

"Night, kianga."

"Night, Ahnou," I echo.

I love you, my heart whispers.

And I swear I hear him repeat these words but know it's just wishful thinking.

Chapter

Twenty

AHNOU

One second, my life is perfect—the next, it's all going to the afterlife.

Nearly six hours have passed since Ender sent me his text before I'm finally able to read it. When I do, every drop of happiness fizzles away.

There's no doubt whatever Ender wants me for is serious if he's calling me into The Veil. I need to depart immediately but loathe to leave Fern alone.

Even though I know she'll be safe out here in the cabin, my inner alpha despises the idea, and I have no way of calling Denine back to me now that she's crossed over.

With great reluctance, I wake my mate. She grumbles, rolling over onto her stomach as she bats my paw.

"Sleep," she groans, and I chuckle at how damn adorable she is.

"Kianga, I have to go, but I will be right back, I promise."

Fern rouses a bit more, her eyelids drooping as she attempts to keep them open. "What's wrong?"

"A friend needs my help. It's nothing bad, I promise, and you'll be safe here. I'll return as quickly as possible. For now, go back to sleep."

She starts to protest, but I bury my snout into the crook of her neck and reposition her so that she's sprawled out on her stomach again.

I rub languid circles around her back until Fern's breathing becomes even with sleep once more.

Then, I give her a kiss atop her mop of glorious red hair and walk outside.

The crisp night air envelops me in its chilly embrace, and I shiver. Although Anubis are covered in fur, it's not dense enough to ward off the cold.

My kind is meant for the desert, not Virginia in late Fall.

Concentrating on the task at hand, I summon a portal into The Veil. At first, nothing happens, and I growl in frustration.

All creatures connected to the afterlife can access The Veil, but since I stay Earth-side, I have no need to channel that part of myself.

While most would find creating a portal a simple task, I struggle to remember what I was taught as a cub.

Finally, I manage to open one big enough to fit my frame. I cast one final glance at the cabin where my mate rests, and then I vanish into thin air.

Seconds later, the portal spits me out into The Veil. It's a strange place that supersedes time and space.

It's neither day nor night, hot nor cold, light nor dark. The Veil simply is—a constant in the universe when everything else changes.

I learned when I came here for camp not to ask too many questions. Even those from The Veil aren't sure how it works.

Not to mention, everyone experiences it differently. Those born of The Veil have a vastly different perspective, as do those who are living versus those who are dead.

It's even more complicated than my conundrum with Fern.

My heart twinges at the thought of her, and I wish I could've brought her with me, but to bring a human into The Veil spells their doom.

Clearing my head, I focus only on Ender. Within seconds, a path forms before me that I know will take me to him.

Luckily, I don't have far to walk before my friend appears before me. He's sitting on a bench, flipping a coin into the air. Next to him sits a box bent out of shape.

"Forgive me, Ender. I hope you haven't been waiting long."

He shrugs. "Who knows?"

"Of course, I forgot that those in The Veil don't keep track. My mate is experiencing some difficulties Earth-side."

Ender cocks his head. "Is she alright?"

"Yes, but someone burned down her house—and her café. Luckily, she was with me, and her friend that lives above the café left before the fire was started there."

"Did they catch the culprit?"

I don't need to tell him this was no coincidence. "Yes. It was Fern's ex-husband. From what I gather from her friend, he's been harassing my mate since…well, forever."

"Do you want me to pay him a visit?"

To many humans, Ender is a form of the Grim Reaper. I grin, thinking about Chet waking up to my friend looming over him.

"Seraphina would be delighted with that idea."

"Who?"

"Fern's friend. She's a Seraphim."

Ender's eyes flash red. "Is she now?"

"Mhmm, it's curious, she's around my mate's age and has no wings."

"How old is your mate?"

"Thirty Earth years, I believe."

"That is interesting. I would like to meet this Seraphim, but we can talk about that later. That these fires were no accident doesn't surprise me after what I've discovered.

Someone has been embezzling money from your mate's café and putting it in an offshore bank. I was able to track and locate it to Panama.

From there, I discovered the account had a safety deposit box, as well. I procured the box with ease, but what I found inside was nothing short of shocking."

Ender picks up the mangled box and hands it to me. It's obvious he wants me to look inside, but I'm too sick with the knowledge that Fern's mother has been stealing from her own daughter.

"Ahnou?"

"Hmm, yes, sorry. Only one person handles my mate's finances. It's her mother."

My friend taps the box, prompting me to open it. It's clear he already knows it's Fern's mother who's behind the offshore account.

When I tip open the lid, the first thing that catches my eye is the sheet of Afterlife Papyrus contained inside.

It's rolled up into a scroll, but I would recognize the special parchment anywhere. It's the only paper in all the worlds that can't be destroyed, and I'm baffled as to how Fern's mother has some.

"Read it. It's a letter to your mate."

Instantly, I balk. "Then it's private and for her eyes only."

Ender nods. "I agree and wouldn't suggest otherwise unless it was of the most dire consequences."

Knowing my friend would never lie to me about something so serious, I unfurl the scroll and scan the words. With every passing sentence, horror settles inside of me.

It's from Fern's father, meant to be given to her after he passed. It chronicles his struggle to keep his wife happy while trying to do what was best for his daughter.

And realizing that he failed.

Mrs. Mabon poisoned her husband's mind, convincing him that if children knew the truth about Fern, she would be ostracized or worse, bullied.

It's clear Mr. Mabon loved Fern dearly and deferred to his wife's assessment of the situation in an attempt to give Fern the best childhood ever.

As time passed, Mr. Mabon never knew how to verbalize the truth to his daughter, and when he became sick, his wife threatened to not let Fern visit if he told her.

But Mr. Mabon circumvented his wife by writing everything down on Afterlife Papyrus, something Mrs. Mabon can never destroy, and then left this letter to his daughter in his will.

Except, it's obvious that Fern never received it, for whatever reason.

She has no clue to its contents or the truth about who she is, and my alpha snarls with rage at this atrocity.

"Are you alright, Ahnou?"

"No. The injustice against my mate is nearly unbearable."

"Are you not happy with what you have learned, though?"

I bark out a humorless laugh. "How can I be happy when this will upend her world?"

"I am sorry, my friend. Your mate's mother is not to be trusted."

"Sadly, Fern already knows this. I must return to her. Thank you for your help. Can you please forward me the records for the offshore account?"

"Of course. Perhaps when everything is sorted, I can come visit and meet your mate and her wingless Seraphim friend."

"You are always welcome. One last favor, can you please open a portal for me?"

Ender smirks. "You never could open them to save your life. Remember the time your ankle got stuck in one? I've never heard anyone howl so loudly."

I ruffle his wings, making him dance away. With a graceful sweep of his hands, a portal twice the size of the one I conjured appears.

Grateful, I tip my head to him before stepping through and back into the cold, Autumn night.

The cabin remains as I left it, as does Fern. I hesitate at the edge of the bed, knowing what I must tell her is of the utmost importance, but I can't bring myself to wake her.

Instead, I curl my long frame around her naked one, tears leaking out of my eyes at the cruelty of Fern's past.

And the one that will become our future.

Chapter

Twenty-One

FERN

I'm having the best dream.

Ahnou and I are in the kitchen where I'm kneading dough to make cookies…and he's kneading my clit and ass to make me come.

Just as things really start to heat up—all the kitchen puns intended—Ahnou bursts my bubble, telling me to wake up.

When I blink my eyes open, his golden gaze warms, the gold liner around his eyes crinkling with his smile.

"Good morning, beautiful."

"You ruined my dream."

"I'm sorry. I wouldn't have woken you if it wasn't important."

This snaps me out of my sensual haze, and I sit up in the bed. The thin sheet does nothing to conceal my curves, and my nipples are doing their damnedest to poke through the material.

The sexy Anubis before me reaches out to tweak one, but to my disappointment, stops himself. I pout a little, and Ahnou chuckles.

"Later, kianga."

"Do you promise?"

"I promise."

"Tell me what's wrong—although I think you should've given me orgasms first. That's how bad news should be broken."

He chuckles but doesn't even lay a claw on me. Instead, he reaches for something on the dresser next to the bed. It's a rolled-up piece of paper that seems vaguely familiar.

I reach for it, as if it's calling me. "What is this?"

"It's a letter from your father that he left to you in his will."

Oh.

OH.

"That's why I recognize it."

"You've seen this before?"

"Yes."

"And you read what was inside?"

I squirm a bit before exhaling against the tightness in my chest. "Actually, no. My mother read it for me.

The truth is, I…can't read. I'm dyslexic. I mean, I can, a little, but I really struggle and generally avoid it. That's why my mom handled all my finances."

Ahnou's gaze softens, mixed with tenderness and sorrow. "And what did she say this paper said?"

"Just my dad's final thoughts and words to me. It's one of those things I wish I could've read on my own, but I was so distraught with grief, I couldn't even focus."

"I know I'm asking a lot, but I want you to try again now. I will help you with any words that you struggle with."

"No, you don't understand. The letters won't stay in place—"

"They swim around the page like they have minds of their own?"

"Yeah, how do you know that?"

"Or sometimes, they're turned on their sides?"

"Yes…"

"I'm dyslexic, too, Fern. What you've battled with, so have I."

"But I've seen you read—you do audits!"

"Yes, but where I am today isn't from a lack of struggle. The difference between you and me is that I was offered resources to help cope with my disability.

Not to mention, no two dyslexic people are alike. We might have similarities, but everyone needs help specifically tailored to their needs.

I hated reading as a kid, but my community goes above and beyond to give young cubs the tools required to thrive in a society based on the written word.

And I'm so happy they did. Reading is one of my favorite pastimes. To think of all the stories I might have missed out on if I wasn't encouraged to keep trying."

"The only person who knew about me is my mom. I'm sure my teachers suspected. I barely passed school. My mother was…*is* ashamed of my disability.

She told me to never tell anyone because they would make fun of me. Kids sometimes already teased me about my weight, so I believed her.

I literally just shared my secret with someone else for the first time in my life. It was Sera only a couple days ago."

"Oh, kianga."

Ahnou bundles me into his arms, and I'm crying before I even know it. All the years of feeling alone and ashamed come pouring out while my fake Anubis boyfriend rocks me.

Knowing what's between us isn't real makes his tenderness even worse because I want nothing in the world more than for Ahnou to be mine.

But when has life ever been fair to me?

I push aside the pity party blowing up in my mind and squeeze Ahnou tighter. Soon, he'll leave, and I need to savor moments like these while I can.

After a while, he pulls back. "There's nothing shameful or wrong with having dyslexia. In fact, it offers a few advantages others don't have, such as being more observant.

I think it's why your café thrives—because you can give it a special edge that others in the same industry lack.

Your empathic nature helps you connect with your customers, and you're creative enough to make new foods and drinks to appeal to people.

Not to mention the success you've accomplished *without* reading. Your problem-solving skills alone are awe-inspiring.

And there's nothing stopping you from getting help. I will be with you every step of the way."

The tension in my chest eases at his support. "Thank you. That's what Sera promised, too."

"Because she's your friend, and she loves you."

I almost blurt out 'do you love me, too' but manage to bite my tongue in time. Instead, I gesture to the letter from my dad.

"Can you please read it? I trust you. I get why you want me to read it, but when I try, I'm so focused on sounding out words and figuring out what they are that by the time I'm done, I don't know what I've read.

Like I read 'the cat has a blue hat', but it takes me so long to get each word out that by the end, I can't remember what the whole sentence says or means."

"Of course, kianga. Firstly, I want to tell you that this parchment is very special. It's called Afterlife Papyrus and can never be destroyed."

I nod, not really understanding as Ahnou pulls out his gold spectacles, and I remind myself something important is happening, and now's not the time to jump the man.

He unrolls the scroll, his long black claws scraping against the material in an attempt to keep it open. Finally, Ahnou starts reading.

"My dearest ladybug, if you're reading this, I've passed on and my heart aches knowing I can't be with you to help ease your pain. Nothing in my life ever brought me as much joy as you did being my daughter. Your smile is brighter than the sun, and your soul is purer than freshly fallen snow. Don't let anyone dim your sparkle. No matter what, promise to be the wonderful, kind woman I've always known who stares at her world in wonder, and not resentment. Bitterness is a dangerous emotion that eats you from the inside out until you're nothing but a husk of unhappiness."

Ahnou pauses, and I look away, knowing my dad was talking about my mom. Even as a kid, I can't recall a time when she was genuinely content.

"Keep going."

"Please know all I've ever wanted for you is to be happy. That's why I've set aside money for you to start the café of your dreams. If anyone can make it happen, it's you. I was never able to help you before this, and that guilt will linger with me long into the afterlife. A parent should always be there to help their child, no matter their age. I have no excuses except that I failed you and hope the money you receive makes amends."

I shake my head, baffled at how my father thinks he ever failed me. No one, aside from his mom—my grandma—and him ever showed me affection.

They listened to me when I spoke, encouraging my dreams instead of calling them silly as my mother often did.

My Anubis continues. "And now, I must tell you something that breaks my heart. I promised your mother I would never tell you but now I realize how wrong that is. This is the only chance I will get and pray only you read this letter. My dearest ladybug, you have monster blood running in your veins. My great-grandmother hailed from Egypt and was an Anubis. She married a visiting Scotsman—from whom you get your beautiful hair. He was called 'Eric The Red'. They had a son, my grandfather, who had your grandma, and then I came along, followed by you.

The only descendant of my great-grandmother who carried the physical traits of an Anubis was her son, who was half. His daughter, your grandma, has a spot on her back where a stunted tail attempted to grow, but otherwise, her features, mine, and yours are wholly human. Even diluted, there are some characteristics we still share. I don't say this to frighten you, but to help you understand that while you may not look like one, you still carry the blood of an Anubis.

Your mother felt that children would treat you differently—unfairly. We never wanted you to stand out for differences you couldn't even see, and so, we decided to not tell anyone. Your grandma disliked the idea, but after she passed, you were already so sad. I couldn't bring myself to hurt you even more by sharing your mom's and my dishonesty. As time moved on, my silence only became more damning. That coupled with your mother's constant criticisms led me to not say anything and just support you as best I could.

You already had so much on your plate, I didn't want to add to it—and now I am heaping it on. I hope you find it in your heart to forgive me and know that your mother and I just wanted you to have a good childhood. The truth is, I never knew much about my Anubis heritage, and I regret that. Maybe you'll embrace this side of your past and even go meet your distant relatives. Whatever you decide, remember that I love you. There's no one in this world like you. Keep being the light those around you need but don't forget to shine the brightest for yourself. Much love, papa."

Ahnou stops reading, and a heavy silence descends around us. We sit on the bed, neither moving, as I internalize my dad's *true* words.

I realize now that when my mom 'read' his letter to me five years ago, she was literally making up every damn word.

Her betrayal cuts far worse than neither of my parents telling me the truth about my bloodline.

My poor brain jumps from one thing to the other, trying to assimilate what I've learned, and I glance at Ahnou, feeling utterly helpless.

"Breathe, kianga. This…is a lot, I know, but nothing we can't get through together."

Bitterness sweeps through me like a windstorm. It's the very thing my father warned me not to be, but it's all I can feel past the pain.

"I appreciate the sentiment, but there is no 'we' between us, is there? Everything is just an elaborate lie meant to infuriate my mother and ex-husband.

So far, that's panned out for me by having everything I hold dear burned to the ground and learning agonizing secrets about my identity."

Ahnou hangs his head. "I'm sorry, truly I am, but I promise that what I feel for you isn't fake. I care for you deeply, Fern, but you need to understand that being part Anubis changes everything between us."

My heart skips a beat.

"Ch-changes things?"

Oh, crap cannoli, please don't tell me we're related.

Chapter
Twenty-Two
AHNOU

My mate's pale face turns even whiter until she resembles the ghosts that once haunted this cabin.

She looks sickly and ready to pass out, and I would give anything right now to see her beautiful blush.

"What's wrong?"

Fern twists the bedsheets between her fingers. "Is this the part where you tell me we're cousins, and I puke all over the freshly-dusted floorboards?"

I squint, trying to figure out how her mind came up with this scenario. Eventually, I give up and just ask.

"Erm, because we're both Anubis?" she says like it's obvious.

"You do understand that there are thousands of Anubis, right? We might not be as plentiful as humans, but we're not related."

"Oh…then what changes between us?"

"I wasn't exactly forthright. The second I bit your neck, I started the mating process. I meant what I said that it was involuntary.

I was so drawn to you that I imprinted without thought, but because I assumed you were human, I figured you would be able to escape the bond.

For Anubis, there is no way to break a mating bond except through death. You would always be my mate, and I would ache for you, but I deserved nothing less for marking you without permission.

Since I thought you were human, I knew you wouldn't feel the bond like I would, and I figured if I moved back to Egypt it would dull the pain of not being with my mate, but then I marked you with my seed…"

"And we had sex."

"Yes, but not just intercourse, which also reinforces the bond, but I fully knotted you. I realize now that my presence triggered your heat, and like a vicious circle, you sent me into a rut.

We imprinted on one another and completed the mating bond. Fern, there's no turning back. It simply can't be undone, and for this, I'm so sorry."

"Why?"

"Because you weren't given a choice, and you deserve no less than to decide your own fate."

"And if I want to be with you?"

I wince. "You cannot imagine how much I wish that was true, but how you feel is tied to our mating link, created without your knowledge.

Your heat makes you crave me, and when that abates, the bond will still do the same thing."

Fern falls quiet but reaches out to cover my paw with her hand, her fingers lacing through mine, a subconscious act on her part to keep us connected.

The very thing I'm trying to explain.

"Ahnou, I hear what you're saying, and I can't refute it, but I think if you took away my heat, your rut, the mating bond—all of it—I would still want to be with you.

I…I love you, and not because of the reason you think I do. I love you because you are kind and patient.

You treat me like I'm the most precious thing in the world and make me feel special and pretty when all my life, I've felt like an outcast.

When I look in a mirror, all I see are flaws, but when I see myself through your eyes, I become so much more.

Being with you makes me happy. It's like I've been lost since my dad passed five years ago, but I've finally found my home again.

You're the person my soul cries out for, the other half that completes me, and I've been in denial this past week about how much I really do need you.

The thought of you leaving breaks my heart. Not because of the bond but because I don't think I can breathe without you by my side. You are my air, and I love you so much it hurts."

Her words speak to the ache inside of me, and my alpha roars. Not howls—*roars*—because he finally knows she's ours and there's no going back.

"Mine," he growls without permission.

"Yours," Fern confirms.

"Fuck, you're too perfect. I need to be inside of you."

My mate keens, dropping the sheet as I dive into the perfection of her body, tracing every curve with my claws and tongue.

When I reach her dripping pussy, I pump her clit with my nose before gently nibbling at the area around the sensitive spot.

Fern squirms, but I pin her spread body to the bed, slurping up the mess she makes all over my face as she comes.

I want to slow down, but my alpha's riding me hard. He wants to seal her to us physically, a reminder that we're already joined for eternity.

Slow down, I caution my alpha when he flips her onto her stomach.

He growls, pointing out that our mate likes it rough. In seconds, I'm out of my clothes, tearing the fabric to shreds.

Damned asshole alpha.

The fucker doesn't even acknowledge my inner hostility, simply lines up my khenen to Fern's entrance and thrusts in all the way to the bands at the base.

Normally, he would grouse about me wearing them instead of my alpha cuff, but he knows how much our mate loves the feel of them.

Once I'm sunk deep inside of Fern, my alpha sighs, some of the edge rolling off of him as he relaxes.

Our omega, he moans, and I startle with the realization that he's right.

Although Fern's blood is diluted, she clearly is still an Omega Anubis. Why I didn't see this before now baffles me.

The amount of slick she creates, her heat and ability to take my knot…

She was created for us, my alpha crows, and for once, I agree.

Underneath me, Fern pushes her ass back, arching her back, and I nearly swell and spill inside of her at the sight.

I remember she likes it when I whisper naughty things to her, so I lean forward, close to her ear, while I begin to fuck her at a pace that'll drive us both crazy.

"My sexy Anubis mate, taking my khenen nice and deep, just like you're going to take my knot, aren't you?"

"Y-yes! Fuck, I loved when you knotted me!"

"Naughty girl, you want me to fill you up and cover you with my cum, don't you? I want to explode all over you and make you lick up every last drop."

I reach under her to toy with her clit. She moans, her pussy squeezing me so tight my heart skips a beat.

Her tight walls flutter, and I know she's close.

"Are you going to be a good girl, and come all over my khenen?"

Instead of answering, my mate's body seizes up, her pussy holding me in a vice grip before she starts spasming in release.

Her orgasm triggers my own, and I slam forward one last time, my knot swelling to lock us together the second it's inside of her.

And then I fucking unload.

My balls draw up, and my alpha keens almost as loudly as Fern as I flood her sweet pussy with my seed.

Her lower stomach begins to bulge with every passing second, her womb coated with my cream, and I shudder at the thought of it taking root.

Yes! Fuck her, mark her, breed her. Ours.

I shush my alpha, knowing our mate is nowhere near being ready to talk about having children, let alone get pregnant.

Patience, I growl, both of us lost in the heady pleasure of the moment. My alpha doesn't even have a rebuttal. Fucker got what he wanted all along and thinks he'll get his way in this, too.

Easing onto the bed, I tug Fern into my side, keeping us connected. My knot refuses to release, and nearly half an hour passes before the swelling subsides.

Even then, my mate seems disinclined to want me to move, so I stay buried in her warmth as she peppers me with questions about Anubis.

After a bit, my khenen hardens once more, and I fuck her again.

And again.

Until we're both too exhausted to move, but I never want this time to end. My alpha smirks, reminding me nothing has to end since she's now ours forever.

Of course he gets the last word.

Chapter Twenty-Three

FERN

Mated.

I never thought I'd want to be with someone after Chet, but somehow I find myself in the most perfect relationship—Ahnou completes me.

We're lying together in bed while he tells me everything there is about Anubis. I have so many questions.

It's almost surreal to think that the blood that runs through Ahnou's veins also is in mine. Obviously, as my father said in his letter, it's very diluted.

Anubis are swift, agile and graceful, and I'm certainly *none* of these. Perhaps the only thing left in my blood is my ability to go into heat, the very thing that brought Ahnou and me together.

Before this moment, I didn't believe in Fate, but I'm thinking maybe she had a hand in everything.

When I was really struggling to get through my divorce, the townspeople from Cedar Peak Heights would stop into the café and offer me words of encouragement.

I'd always been there for them, they said, and in return, they came to support me. Their kindness gave me the buoyancy to keep going, even if I didn't put much stock into what they said.

But now I understand the clichéd advice about the light at the end of the tunnel, or how all the doors kept closing so the perfect one could open.

Ahnou is the light to my darkness, and all the doors in my life were shutting so that I could finally open the one leading to him.

A small huff of stunned laughter escapes me, and my mate nuzzles the side of my neck. "What are you thinking about?"

"Mushy stuff."

"I suppose it's better than thinking of depressing things."

"Well, speaking of depressing things…" My Anubis groans, making me giggle. "It's not that bad, I just want to talk about my mom."

"That's *very* bad."

I roll my eyes. "Listen, I'm not quite sure what to do about everything I've learned. Ideally, I'd like to never speak to the woman again.

But just thinking about that makes me want to be sick—I think my dad's haunting me to make sure I keep my promise to him."

The last bit is a joke, but Ahnou pulls back from me. I crane my head to look at him, his expression aghast.

"When did you make a promise to your father and what was it?"

"Um, right before he died, he asked me to take care of my mom and never leave her. I swore I would because we only had each other left."

Ahnou's golden eyes widen, and he throws himself back on the pillows. It's the most dramatic thing I've ever seen the man do.

"What's wrong?" I demand, poking his rock-hard stomach.

It's literally the antithesis of the gelatinous jiggle of mine.

"You made a Death Vow with your father."

"A what?"

"A Death Vow. When one Anubis asks another to do something as their final wish, the living Anubis is upheld to maintain it until one of the living parties involved dies."

"Wait, wait, wait…so you're saying I can never escape my mother because of the thing I promised my father?

And the only way I'll ever be rid of the woman hell bent on making me unhappy is if either she or I die?!"

"Yes."

All my contentment from earlier drifts away. I'm so damned exhausted by the roller coaster of emotions—the constant highs to the plummeting lows.

My mind and body are about to crash.

Ahnou pulls himself together and rolls back into me. "Do you want to squeeze in between my shirt and fur again?"

"You're not wearing a shirt."

"I can put one on."

The idea certainly has merit.

"Do I have any options that don't involve either my mom or me dying?"

"Eh…we can try moving. The further the distance we put between us, the less of an effect she'll have on you, but it might also make you very sick.

It's hard to say since both you and your father are not full Anubis. Not to mention now that you're bonded to me, that should help strengthen any tension you would feel at being separated from your mother."

On the one hand, I love the idea of being away from her, but on the other, I adore Cedar Peak Heights—not that there's anything left for me there.

Ahnou continues. "I think the best course of action for now is when we return to Denine's house, we call the insurance company and file a claim.

Ideally, I would like you to file something with the police about your mother's involvement, but I understand if this is too much for you.

Either way, I will still need to file your taxes, but they can be amended later on. The government is much more likely to be lenient on you if you have legal documentation of the embezzlement."

Good grief, when I asked the universe to help me with my taxes, I didn't mean to make it this complicated, but if it comes with an Anubis…

"It's just a suggestion, kianga. Whatever you're most comfortable with, I will defer to. We'll find a way to make everything work, I promise."

All day long, he's reminded me that I don't have to go on this path alone anymore, that I have him, Sera, Francine, and the people of Cedar Peak Heights behind me.

Why I'm just realizing this now, I don't know. For the longest time, I felt all I had was my mom and Chet—maybe that's why I clung to him for so long.

"I have a favor to ask," Ahnou says, interrupting my thoughts.

"Anything."

"That's a dangerous thing to promise," he teases.

"Like you would ever ask me to do anything bad."

He tips back his head, laughing. "I just had a similar conversation with my friend Ender. I would like for you to meet him."

"Is that your favor?"

"No, I wanted to know…if you'll come to Egypt with me."

"Of course! I would love to!"

"You can meet my parents and my sisters who still live over there as well as my cousins."

"I wish I had more family to introduce you to, but I really only had my grandma, my dad's mom.

My mother's parents stopped speaking to her after she married my dad. I can't help but wonder if maybe that's the source of her resentment. Neither of my parents ever seemed to truly love one another."

Ahnou sighs. "I can't imagine how very sad that was for you growing up, and the impression it must have left on you.

For Anubis, mating is—generally—a very special process that can't happen accidentally…like it did between us. I'm beginning to think it was no accident at all."

I smile up at him. "I agree. So when would you like to go to Egypt?"

"In February. It's the Festival of The Wag, which honors Osiris and those who have gone into the afterlife.

Tax season doesn't really begin until April here in the States. Although I audit all year round, I usually ask for February off.

It's too cold for me unless I'm far south, and I like to go back and be with my family. I so very rarely meet other Anubis."

"That sounds good to me. And now that I don't have my café, I need to figure out what I want to do. I'm sure I'll have enough insurance money to rebuild it, but that'll take time."

"Time is something I think both of us will have. I had another audit after you, but I've already requested for it to be transferred to someone else.

I told them your case was going to take longer. We can relax here in Cedar Peak Heights over the holidays and then travel in February. Perhaps I can celebrate some human traditions with you."

"What do you mean?"

"Like Thanksgiving."

"You've never done Thanksgiving before?"

"No. I really don't have any friends here in the States. I have a house that I go to in between audits and during the down season, but the majority of my time is spent traveling and living out of hotels."

I wrinkle my nose. "Ew…I'm sorry! That was rude of me."

Ahnou laughs. "Nah, just honest. It's not the most glamorous lifestyle, but I'm an introvert and keep to myself. It's never bothered me until now. With you in my life, I don't want to be alone."

"Then it's settled! You'll have your very first Thanksgiving with me."

He grins. "My first kiss. My first Thanksgiving. I'm looking forward to sharing all my firsts with you."

I blush at the implication, even though it wasn't anything naughty. My mate growls, sensing my arousal, and pulls me closer to him.

A shriek escapes when he nips at my neck when suddenly he goes stock still. He stares at the door, one ear twitching before finally relaxing.

"Is everything all right?"

"I thought I heard something, but I couldn't hear over your screeching."

"Har-har." I smack his bicep playfully. "It's *your* fault because you're the one who made me do it!"

We start tussling again when Ahnou stops once more. He gets out of the bed and quickly throws on his jeans just as the bedroom door slams open.

There, in the dim shaft of the moonlight from the window, I see my mother. Her hair is in disarray and her expression is crazed.

But what scares me the most is the metal I see glinting in her hand.

Chapter
Twenty-Four
AHNOU

My heart seizes in my chest.

Fern's mom stands before us, holding a gun, cocked and ready. I have no doubt that it's loaded, too.

I want to go to my mate, but thankfully, the weapon isn't pointed at her—it's leveled directly at me.

There's no doubt of Mrs. Mabon's intention, but it makes me feel better to have the gun aimed at me.

"M-mom!" Fern stutters. "Put the gun down."

"No. If you had just listened, none of us would be in this situation—and now I have to take care of it the only way possible."

"Shooting someone isn't the only way!"

Poor Fern is trying, but there's no point in attempting to reason with Mrs. Mabon. She's too far gone in her own fear to be logical.

Her next words confirm this. "Don't you see—I was just trying to help you."

The sheer desperation in the other woman's voice tells me that she believes it.

She really thinks she was helping Fern all this time by hiding her dyslexia, her Anubis heritage, and encouraging her relationship with Chet.

And in an attempt to shield her daughter from the very things she was worried about, she made Fern miserable.

"Do you know that this *monster* broke into my bank and stole what wasn't his?!"

"Ahnou, what is she talking about?"

"When I was doing your taxes, I came across some withdrawals that didn't add up. The further I dug into your records, I realized something was wrong.

I had a friend help. He discovered an offshore account that was embezzling money from your café—small amounts here and there that added up over the years.

The owner of the bank account revealed your mother's name. It's where the Afterlife Papyrus was being stored."

"Thief!" Mrs. Mabon bellows.

Neither Fern nor I point out that she is also one—if not more so—but it's clear the woman is unwell and teetering on the edge of sanity.

My hope is that she doesn't tip over the ledge and pull the trigger.

As if sensing my thoughts, Fern's mother squints at me. "Why were you doing my daughter's taxes?"

Again, Fern and I say nothing, but Mrs. Mabon finally connects all the dots. Considering how I showed up on the same day that Fern called her mom to tell her about her tax woes.

"You're the auditor!"

It always seemed so obvious to me, but Mrs. Mabon looks absolutely gobsmacked at the idea that I'm not Fern's real boyfriend. Her expression melts from shock to disgust.

"You've been sleeping with this monster that you just met?! I knew it—I knew it! You're an Anubis whore!

Your genes came shining through, alright. I told your father this was what we could expect!

You're all nothing but a bunch of filthy, promiscuous creatures…and I'm ending this right now."

My mate screams as her mother fires the gun. I'm quick enough to dodge a bullet, but I'm so hyper-focused on making sure that I do that I miss seeing Fern lunge in my direction.

She catapults into my body, knocking me to the ground, and the bullet meant for me lodges itself inside Fern's chest.

Instantly, she collapses to the ground, and Mrs. Mabon screams so loudly that I clap a hand over an ear as I rush to my mate's side.

Her mother falls to her knees and crawls over to Fern, too, sobbing hysterically. "No! Please, no! I'm so sorry! It wasn't meant for you! It wasn't meant for you!"

The distraught woman repeats this over and over until finally she grasps my hand and begs me to save her daughter.

Calling upon everything inside of me, I focus and open up a portal, dragging Fern with me into The Veil, leaving behind the echo of her mother's wails.

Here, Fern's death will be slower, but if I don't get her help soon, die she will.

I conjure a mental image of Ender, and a path erupts before me that I race down until I come to a strange cottage.

When I knock on the door, my friend steps out, and I thrust Fern into his arms. "Please save my mate!"

Ender cocks his head, his sightless eyes flashing red. "She is on the brink of death, but there is nothing you or I can do.

Death can only beget more death. What you need is someone who can bring life. Do you know anyone?"

Without hesitation, I open another portal and rocket myself into Cedar Peak Heights, in front of Francine's house.

I dash up the steps of her porch, pounding on her door like a madman. To my relief, Seraphina answers.

"Please, it's an emergency—you must come with me into The Veil."

"The what?"

I realize the Seraphim has no idea what I'm talking about, but I have no time to explain. Instead, I take her hand, reopen the portal, and jump in.

This time, we come out exactly where I left Ender. He still stands there, cradling my mate and rocking her gently.

My friend places her back in my arms while I weep, and Seraphina sinks to her knees, her face coated in tears.

"F-fern?! What happened to her?"

"Her mother came to the cabin. She meant to shoot me, but Fern jumped in front of the bullet."

"Oh gods," the Seraphim chokes, watching the blood flow slowly from the center of my mate's chest. "What can we do?"

"The Veil will slow her death, but if she cannot be given life, she won't survive," Ender explains.

"Ender and I are entities of death. We help those cross over into the afterlife, not help them to live.

But you are Seraphim. You are the very definition of giving life to others. And so, I beg of you, please give my mate life again."

Seraphina sucks in a sharp breath. "I never, ever wanted to be what I am, and have actively avoided ever doing anything to earn my wings…

But for Fern, I would die myself. Tell me what I must do."

I look at Ender and the Teraphim nods. "Place your hands over your friend's heart. What do you feel?"

"Erm…nothing. Just her very faint heartbeat. Oh, wait! I feel a pulse of power!"

"Yes. That power is you. Connect that feeling to your hands and push it into your friend."

"I don't think—"

"You don't need to think, you need to *feel*. Let the love that you have for her guide you with this."

Seraphina closes her eyes. Within seconds, her hands begin to glow a beautiful gold that swells and crests, getting bigger until it nearly blinds me.

When I can see again, Fern is no longer bleeding and the pulse at her neck grows stronger.

The Seraphim stands, but her body is too weak from the gift that she's given to my mate, and Ender catches her just as she falls.

A gurgle of pain escapes her lips as her body spasms in agony. She twitches and writhes in my friend's arms.

"Ender, what's happening?"

"Her wings are being born."

He sets her on the ground where the Seraphim curls into a ball. My friend rubs up and down, as if coaxing the dormant feathers free.

With every passing second, Fern's breathing becomes steady, her heartbeat resuming its familiar rhythm.

My mate stirs and then jackknifes upright in my arms just as Seraphina screams as the Seraphim's mouth opens and a deluge of light spews forth.

A crackle of power knocks us all backward, and when I look again, Fern's friend is lying in a pool of her own blood with giant white wings cascading down her back.

They're even larger than Ender's and speckled red. Everyone gasps, and then Seraphina faints.

Fern trembles in my arms at the sight, and I drink in every movement, relief coursing through my veins.

Thank Osiris, my mate survived.

Chapter

Twenty-Five

FERN

I'm trapped in a strange dream, and when I finally wake up, the world is covered in blood.

Strong hands hold me back when I try to lean forward. I turn to find Ahnou holding me. His face is set in hard lines, his gaze panicked. With a trembling hand, I reach up to cup his snout.

He stares at me for a few more moments before the tension releases from his shoulders. Then he nuzzles his nose along my face.

"Kianga, speak to me. How do you feel?"

His question makes no sense, but I quickly scan my body, assessing to see.

"Ow, my chest hurts," I wince, rubbing at it, only to find it sticky with blood.

My blood.

"What happ—"

My question is cut off by a long, low moan. Peering in the direction of the sound, I spy a quivering mess of red and white nearby.

"What's that?"

"It's your friend," a strange voice speaks.

A shadow steps into view, and a monster I've never seen before bends down. "Hello, mate of Ahnou, I am Ender. And this is your friend, the Seraphim."

It takes me a moment to realize he's talking about Sera. Confused, I try to pull out of Ahnou's hold again, but he won't let me go.

I look around wildly, not recognizing where I am. This isn't the cabin, nor is it Cedar Peak Heights. I don't understand why Serafina is here, nor why we're covered in so much blood.

"A-Ahnou," I stammer, my teeth chattering together.

He rubs up and down my arms vigorously until my body warms. "It's going to be okay. Do you remember anything?"

"N-no."

My mind is hazy, my memories dancing away from me like the letters on the page when I tried to read.

After a moment, I mumble this, and Ahnou shoots his friend a worried look, but the strange monster waves it off.

"Don't fret—she died. Things are going to be a little murky for a bit."

I…died?!

My pulse speeds up as I try to remain calm. Ahnou returns to nuzzling my neck, exhaling a happy sigh.

"That's the most beautiful sound I've ever heard."

"What is?"

"Your heartbeat, your pulse. It tells me that you're living. We came so close to losing you."

Haltingly, he recounts the story of how my mother found us at the cabin and tried to shoot him, but I jumped in front of Ahnou first.

My Anubis mate tries to scold me and ends up just licking at my ears, too happy that I'm okay now to be mad at me.

"So where are we?"

"The Veil. Most people liken it to the afterlife. It's not entirely, but it's connected to it. Entities linked to life and death can enter. Those who are not do not survive.

By bringing you into The Veil, I slowed your death until I could find someone who could help you."

"She did die," Ahnou's friend, Ender, adds.

"You keep saying that, and I don't understand. If I died, how am I alive?"

"Because of Serafina," my mate answers, pointing toward the dual-toned blob of white and red.

It hasn't moved the entire time Ahnou spoke, and I realize that it really is supposed to be Serafina.

Ender explains what she did to save me and my mouth drops open. "Oh, no, no, no. Sera never wanted to be a Seraphim! She's avoided getting her wings her entire life!"

"Your friend had a choice to make—stay the same and let you die, or give you life and get her wings.

Her sacrifice is one of the greatest things a Seraphim can do in terms of giving life. It's why her wings are so large—the bigger the act of creating life, the larger the wings.

But because of it, she has borne much pain to free them. The bones in her body must reshape to accommodate these new appendages."

I gasp at Ender's words, guilt swamping me, but Ahnou gives me a squeeze.

"Seraphina loves you dearly. She didn't do anything you wouldn't do."

He's right, but I sob at the sacrifice Sera made for me, knowing it's not what she wanted and hating how much pain it's caused her.

"Will she be all right? Do we need to take her to a doctor?"

"The Seraphim will be fine and will heal soon. Her back had to reform itself and regrow new bones."

Bile rises up my throat, and I gag at the mental image of Sera sprouting wings. It's not angelic like I would have thought.

It was bone shattering and harrowing, and I can't even begin to fathom the amount of power—life—she poured into me if I was truly dead.

Staring at the massive amount of white feathers before me, I have no idea how Sera will function, let alone walk.

I whisper this worry, and Ender chuckles. "She'll do what she was always meant to do—*fly*."

Ahnou continues to stroke my arms. "Don't fret, kianga. Seraphina will be alright."

"Where…where is my mother?"

"She's back at the cabin. Ender went Earthside for a moment to call the police. I'm sure by now she's in custody."

The thought should've saddened me, or even made me feel sick to know that I wouldn't be able to take care of her when she goes to jail, but instead. I don't feel anything.

Slivers of my conversation with Ahnou right before my mom burst into the cabin come back, and I wonder…

"Did I *really* die?"

"Ender says you did. I think I was too distraught to see the truth before me, clinging to the desperate hope that you would be ok."

"Don't you see what that means?! If I died, that means the Death Vow I made with my father is over!"

My mate blinks his large golden eyes slowly, exhaling a deep breath. "You're right. You're free, Fern! You're finally free of her."

The most beautiful relief crashes through me, and I swear I'm euphoric at the knowledge that I'm no longer emotionally tied to someone who spent my entire life hurting me.

Suddenly, the pile of feathers shifts. In a flash, Ender bends down to help Sera into a sitting position.

Her face is chalky and her expression is dazed as she tries to find her equilibrium—no small feat with the monstrous forms behind her back.

This time when I lean forward, Ahnou lets me go. I crawl over to Sera and wrap my arms gently around her waist.

"You saved my life and scared the poop out of me!"

Seraphina inhales, the sound rattling in her chest alarmingly. "Don't blame your incontinence on me. Besides, I didn't do anything you wouldn't do for me."

Of course, she's cracking jokes, but I take this as a sign she's going to be ok.

"Are you in pain?"

"No. How about you?"

"Surprisingly, I'm doing okay for someone who was shot in the chest."

I rub the area in question, glad to find the skin stitched up since I don't handle blood and guts very well, as I stare at Seraphina in awe.

"This probably isn't the best time, but your wings are the most beautiful thing I've ever seen."

"Even more beautiful than Ahnou's cock?"

Stumbling back in embarrassment, I clap a hand to my cheeks. Ender crouches down, his eyes flashing an eerie crimson.

"Why are you looking at Ahnou's cock?"

Seraphina shrugs and then groans at the obvious pain it causes her. "I'm not—but Fern's told me about it."

I blush brighter than the red caking my boobs that my brain just now registers are bared for the world—er, Veil—to see.

With a shriek, I attempt to cover myself, but there's just too much of me to accomplish this. Thankfully, my mate wraps himself back around me.

"It's okay. No one is looking."

His words don't really make me feel better, but I pat his arm, telling him I appreciate the gesture. "Can we find a blanket or something, please?"

"How about we go back to Denine's house? Serafina is going to stay here with Ender while he takes care of her."

"No, she's not," my best friend argues.

"Yes, she is," Ender counters.

"Just try and stop me!"

The other man snorts. "I won't have to—your wings will. They're too big, and you're too inept at using them to get anywhere. Accept your fate and it will be easier."

Wow…I can't believe this guy just told Sera to accept her fate—a Seraphim who fought her entire existence to avoid creating life just so she couldn't have wings.

"He's in for a rough battle," I whisper to Ahnou.

"Don't worry, Ender won't do anything to hurt your friend."

I snort. "I'm not worried about him hurting her, but the other way around!"

My mate chuckles. "Come on, let's go get you cleaned up. Maybe we can make it through one night without anything bad happening."

"That sounds divine. I want to sleep for thirty years!"

"As long as you're by my side, I'll do anything with you."

He gives me a kiss, and I sigh in contentment.

They say nothing is certain but death and taxes, and I'll be damned if the two didn't bring me my happily ever after.

Chapter
Twenty-Six
AHNOU

Fern bounces up and down in excitement as I set down the last dessert…all sixteen of them, but when your mate's a baker, it's to be expected.

Dessert makes me think of Fern in nothing but an apron, whipping up my favorite treat—cream from her pussy.

As if reading my thoughts, my sweet redhead elbows me in the stomach, grunting when I don't even flinch.

"Behave."

"I don't know what you're talking about."

"The front of your pants are straining."

"That's just the pants."

My mate snorts back a giggle as she cups my khenen through the fabric. "Maybe if you're a good boy, I'll let you lick me somewhere later."

I scowl while my tail wags obnoxiously back and forth, silently expressing my excitement.

"How am I supposed to calm down when you say things like that?"

"Well you better figure it out because here comes Francine."

Thankfully, this cools my ardor enough that I don't have to hold anything in front of me like a randy cub.

"Are you ready for your first Thanksgiving, young man?" she asks, eyeing the sweet treats Fern made.

"As ready as I'll ever be."

"Good. Now go open the door. I believe Fern is expecting some visitors."

I nod but wonder who Fern invited. Aside from Seraphina and Francine, everyone else in Cedar Peak Heights is celebrating with their family.

We asked the ladies to come over to Denine's house since neither has anyone else to enjoy the meal with, and I knew Fern was going to cook up a storm.

Perhaps my mate invited Ender…

But then I shake my head, negating the thought. Ever since Seraphina returned from The Veil, she's changed—the mere mention of my friend makes her moody and sullen.

Whatever happened between the two of them didn't end well, but considering how Ender is really the only friend I have in this area, I'm not sure who could be at the door.

My jaw drops when I open it to find my family—my parents, sisters, their mates, and all my nieces and nephews.

I stare in shocked wonder as they push their way in, each giving me a hug, all of our tails wagging.

"Happy Thanksgiving, son!" my mother crows like it's a holiday she's celebrated her entire life.

"Happy Thanksgiving!" my dad parrots.

"Are you surprised?" a voice asks behind me, and I turn and yank my mate into my arms. I give her a kiss that borderlines inappropriate before she wiggles out of my arms.

"Hello, Mr. and Mrs. Napa, I'm Fern."

"Please, call us Mom and Dad. It's so wonderful to have another daughter!"

Fern grins, tears filling her eyes, and I have no doubt that she'll take up my mother's offer. With her own mother in jail, my mate's just started putting together the pieces of her life.

All she's ever wanted was to be loved and supported, and slowly but surely, she's pulling the right people into her life and finally surrounding herself with her pack.

My sisters push forward, each talking over the other, their mates resigned to the fact that they'll never get a word in edgewise.

While they pepper Fern with questions, I crouch down on one knee as my nephews tackle me to the ground. Next to us, my nieces try to convince me to let them do a makeover on me.

"Did someone say makeover?" Serafina breezes into the room, one large wing knocking off a painting on the wall.

She curses under her breath before righting it. "Sorry. Still getting used to these things. I bet Auntie Fern will let you do a makeover on her, and me, too."

"Ooooh, Thanksgiving makeovers, how fun! We'll do that after we bake cookies."

All the kids cheer while I groan. "No more cookies!"

"What's wrong with cookies?" my dad demands.

"She's already made twelve dozen!"

My sister, Nephthys, rolls her eyes, her expression teasing. "That didn't mean you had to sit down and eat them all at once!"

I snort. "You obviously have never tried any of my mate's cookies."

"I would have—if there were any left!"

Fern laughs. "There's plenty of sweets, I promise. As Ahnou suggested, I might have gone overboard. I wanted to make sure everyone had a variety of options.

Aside from the traditional options of turkey, stuffing, cranberry sauce, sweet potato casserole, pecan pie, and pumpkin pie, I made ham, roast beef, and green bean casserole.

Not to mention a couple cakes, cookies, cupcakes, and a few other pies. Oh, and dinner rolls, too."

Nephthys' mate wipes an imaginary tear from his eye. "Thanksgiving sounds like The Afterlife."

This makes Fern chuckle. "I never imagined saying it that way. We say something similar—that something is like heaven."

"Not to us Anubis."

She beams at my words, knowing I mean her, too.

"Everyone ready to eat?" Francine calls from the dining room.

Without hesitation, my family heads toward the back of the house where I formally introduce Seraphina and Francine.

While everyone oohs and ahhs over the food on the table, I come up behind my mate and wrap her up in a bear hug.

"Thank you. How did you arrange this?"

"Remember when Sera asked for your mom's email? She was actually getting it for me. Your mom and I have been talking for a couple of weeks.

I explained how excited you were for your first Thanksgiving, and the next thing I knew, we were arranging for your whole family to come over and experience it!

The best part—Sera only helped a little! I did most of the reading and writing to your mom. Those classes I've been taking have really opened my eyes to what I'm capable of."

"Have I ever told you how amazing you are? You sound so proud of yourself, and you should be. You're one in a million, Fern Mabon, don't ever forget it."

My mate beams up at me as she stretches on her tippy toes, our mouths meeting somewhere in between when Francine clears her throat.

"Are you two lovebirds done canoodling? We have a dinner to start!"

Fern chokes back a laugh, trying to look repentant as she directs everyone to a chair and helps Seraphina take off the lids of the various dishes.

Steam clouds the air, filling the room with delectable scents that make my stomach rumble. I want to dig in, but Seraphina shoos me back when I reach for a serving spoon.

"Wait! First, Fern wants to read something."

This immediately gets my attention and quells my hunger.

My sweet redhead twitches as all eyes swivel to her, and she twists a hand in her skirt before pulling out a piece of paper.

Huh, skirts with pockets.

"As you all know, my house and café were burnt down. It was very hard for me because all of my precious gifts from my grandma and dad were destroyed, too.

But Ahnou had taken boxes of my financial records here to Denine's house to scan, and by some stroke of luck, my grandma's cookbook was in one of the boxes.

When he showed it to me, I bawled for like an hour. Poor Ahnou was a mess trying to figure out what was wrong and how to fix it."

Everyone at the table laughs while my sister's mates and dad give a look. They know my pain because they can't stand it when their mates cry, either.

Fern continues. "Since I've always struggled to read, I learned to memorize my grandma's recipes.

This was no hardship as I have a great memory and I love to bake. I've made these recipes so many times, I could do it in my sleep.

But because I never tried to read anything before, I didn't realize how much I was missing out on.

This cookbook isn't just full of recipes, but also stories from my grandma's past, as well as some poems she wrote.

Being able to read them is almost as miraculous as still having this book, and I cherish both so much.

So, in honor of my grandma and not letting dyslexia hold me back anymore, I would like to read everyone a poem before we dig in."

My mate holds out the piece of paper, squinting a bit before relaxing. She glances up at me briefly, and I give her a smile, hoping she knows how much I love her.

When Fern finishes, everyone claps and whistles, and her face flushes the lovely strawberry red that I love so much.

Seraphina gives her a one-armed hug and then gestures at my parents and siblings to help themselves.

Soon, the room is full of forks and knives clanking against the fancy plates Francine brought over as my nieces and nephews vie for Fern's attention.

My dad, sitting to my left, catches my eye. "Is tonight still the big night?" He asks this in a whisper, and I nod.

My parents know I have something special planned, made even more so by the fact that they're able to experience it with me.

After everyone is ready to explode, I stand up. "Can we all take a moment to thank Fern, Seraphina, and Francine for this amazing meal?"

Again, the table erupts in cheers and whistles while the three women grin. I raise a paw for silence while walking over to Fern.

I tug her out of the chair until she's standing. She stares up at me in confusion while I dig around in my pocket.

"One more thing." I fall to one knee like I practiced over and over. "Fern Mabon, will you marry me?"

Popping open the lid on the box, I reveal a golden Egyptian wedding band, engraved with an ankh and Egyptian lotuses.

Fern's hand flies to her mouth. "But we're mated! I mean, I guess I didn't think Anubis got married…"

"It's a human thing, but you're human, too, and since you were primarily raised as such, I know how important a wedding probably is to you.

Your first marriage wasn't a happy one, so I thought we could replace those bad memories with some new ones—better ones."

"Yes!" she shrieks, throwing herself into me so that I fall backwards as my nieces and nephews howl in happiness.

Somehow, I manage to get the ring slipped onto her finger since she won't stop peppering my face with kisses.

When we stand, all the women in the room crowd my mate to look at the ring. Her friend demands to be the Maid of Honor, and Francine wants to know when we're getting 'hitched'.

Fern taps her cheek. "In the fall, I think. It's my favorite time of year, plus it'll give me time to plan as well as get back on my feet."

The insurance company already gave my mate the money she needed to start rebuilding her café. As for her house, we're taking our time deciding what to do since Francine said we could stay at Denine's.

"Well, I do hope you have cubs before then!" my mom exclaims, and Fern promptly starts choking.

"Usually that doesn't happen until after the wedding," she croaks, and Francine cackles.

"Not with the way you two go at it!"

The familiar red creeps back into my mate's cheeks. "We'll see."

Instantly, visions of Fern naked and rounded with my baby make me hard. I cough and turn quickly, pretending to check my phone when I see I have a text message from Ender.

I'm waiting outside.

Excusing myself, I go to the front door and step out. There, in the corner of the porch, is my winged friend.

The air is so cold that I can see both our breaths, and I hate the chilly temperature, but I don't want to invite him in—not with Seraphina inside.

"I apologize. We're celebrating Thanksgiving, and I didn't see your text. Is everything alright?"

Ender hums. "Yes, everything's fine. I'm just calling in on that favor."

"Oh…ok. What can I do for you?"

"I need you to help me kidnap someone."

A bark of laughter bursts forth from me. "That's hilarious. You delivered it so blandly, I almost thought you were serious…"

His expression never changes, and my heart sinks with the realization that he *is* serious.

"Ender, I can't help you kidnap someone! Are you crazy? I just resigned from the IRS, but they have all my information. I'm not exactly a low-profile person to them."

"They won't know, and besides, we'll be going to The Veil."

I groan, the situation getting worse by the second. Licking my lips, I demand to know who he wants to take.

"The Seraphim."

"Fern's best friend?!"

"The very same."

"She hates you."

"I know."

I scrape a hand between my ears and laugh. "Your funeral, mate, but I'm not taking the Seraphim against her wishes."

Just then, the front door opens and out steps Fern.

"Oh, hi, Ender! Happy Thanksgiving!"

My friend bows to her. "And to you. I apologize for interrupting. Ahnou and I were just discussing the terms of his favor."

"We'll talk later, but I don't think I can help with this."

Fern frowns. "Maybe I can help."

"No!" I shout at the same time Ender deadpans, "I want to kidnap the Seraphim."

Her expression smooths into something too blank for me to decipher, and I want to shake Ender for his foolishness, but then, my mate begins to laugh.

And laugh.

And laugh.

Ender and I exchange confused looks. "What's so funny, Fern?"

"Oh, nothing. Tell me, Ahnou, did you promise Ender you would help him?"

"Erm, yes."

"Well, Anubis don't go back on their word."

"Are…are you encouraging me to help him kidnap your friend?!"

My mate shrugs. "What can I say, I want her to have the same happiness I have, but Sera is way too stubborn to acknowledge the truth."

"And what's that?" Ender asks.

"That's for you both to figure out."

He nods before checking his phone. "I'll text you the plans." Then, he opens a portal and disappears.

"Fern—"

She doesn't even give me time to speak, just pushes me against the side of the house and rubs her perfect breasts back and forth across my stomach.

"Be a good boy and promise you'll help Ender."

I hiss as she lowers herself onto her knees, her tits propping up my hardening khenen through my pants.

"You can't do that!"

"Can, too!"

"My alpha is going to spank your ass!"

"Good—that's what I want. Right after you do everything I say, first."

I smirk, loving the dynamic of our relationship and how easily we switch back and forth, feeding off one another's pleasure.

"We should probably head back inside," I murmur with regret.

"Yeah…but maybe you warm me up first."

"Everyone will smell you."

"Crap, fine, but promise me you'll knot me the first chance you get."

Yanking her back upright, I kiss my mate with all the love I have for her in my heart. "I promise."

And an Anubis never breaks a promise.

About
The
Author

Wendi Gogh is a twenty-something free spirit
who writes to the beat of the Monster Mash.
She loves inclusive, diverse love, and of
course, happily ever afters.
When she's not writing, Wendi likes to read
Mary Shelley (her favorite monster author) and watch
The Office. Bears, Beets, Battlestar Galactica.

ALSO BY THE AUTHOR

Monstrous Meet Cutes©

Audited By The Anubis

Bossed By The Boggart

Claimed By The Cthulhu

Checked Out By The Chupacabra

Dared By The Dagon

Edged By The Erlking

Friendzoned By The Frankendoll

Ghosted By The Gorgon

Hogtied By The Hodag

Inked By The Ithaqua

Jinxed By The Jaculus

Kissed By The Kiwakwa

Lured By The Letiche

Marked By The Marid

Nailed By The Nagual

Oiled By The Onglo

Pucked By The Puca

Phished By The Phadua

Queened By The Qarins

Rewarded By The Rainbow Serpent

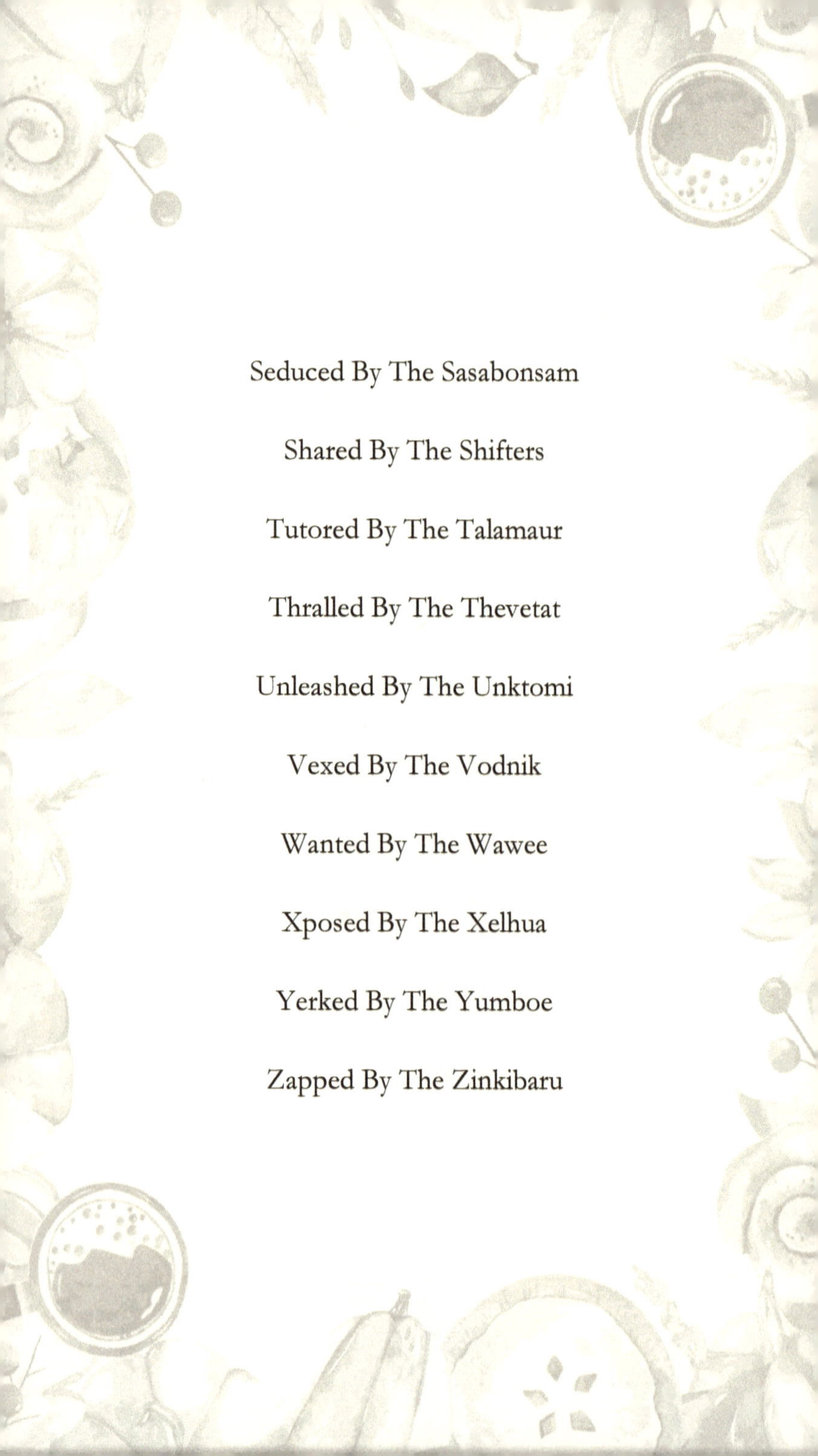
Seduced By The Sasabonsam

Shared By The Shifters

Tutored By The Talamaur

Thralled By The Thevetat

Unleashed By The Unktomi

Vexed By The Vodnik

Wanted By The Wawee

Xposed By The Xelhua

Yerked By The Yumboe

Zapped By The Zinkibaru

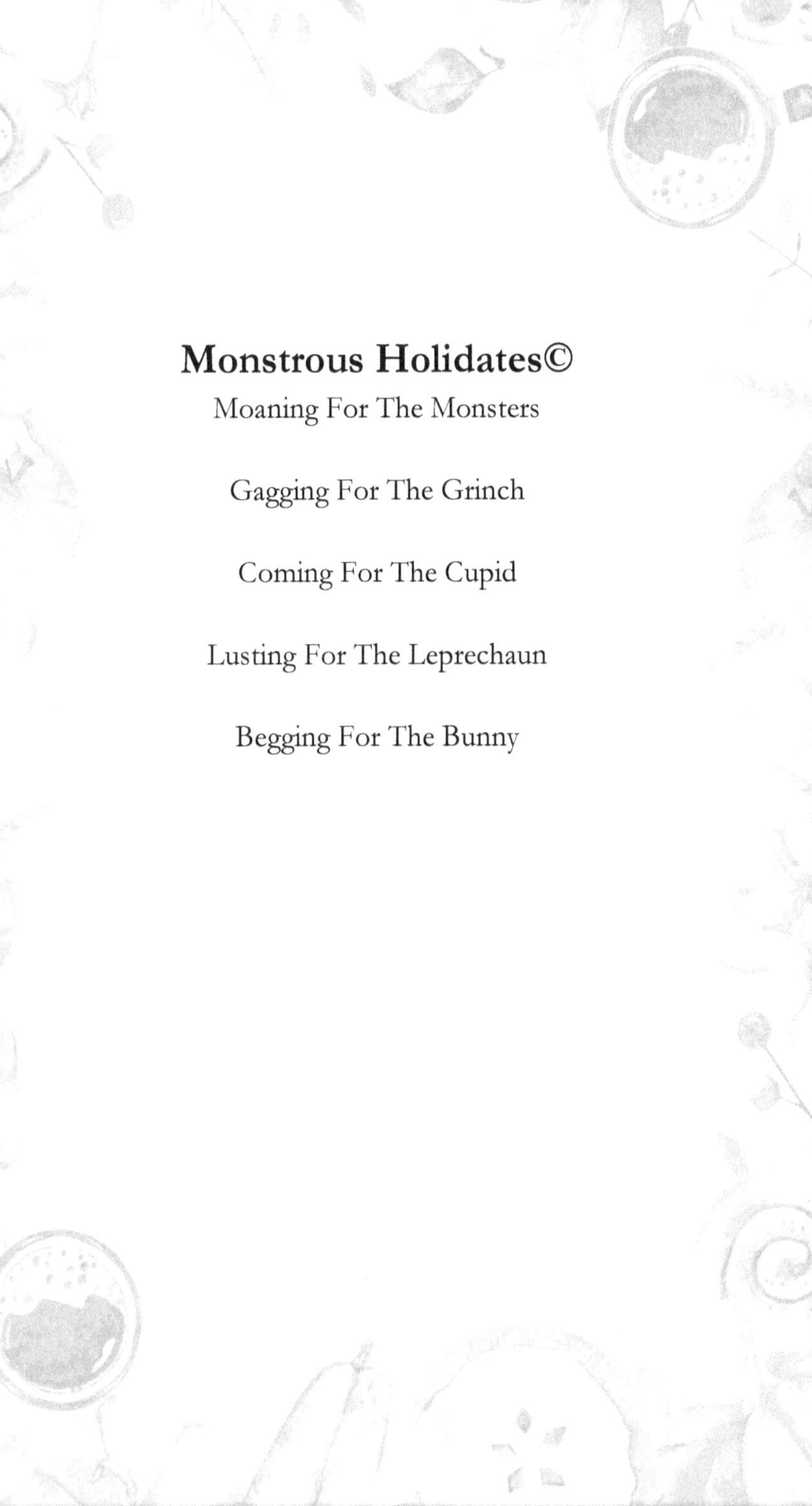

Monstrous Holidates©

Moaning For The Monsters

Gagging For The Grinch

Coming For The Cupid

Lusting For The Leprechaun

Begging For The Bunny